DEVILFISH

JOHN LEE SCHNEIDER

SEVERED PRESS
HOBART TASMANIA

DEVILFISH

Copyright © 2021 John Lee Schneider

WWW.SEVEREDPRESS.COM

ISBN: 978-1-922551-73-3

"Men may sail the seas for a lifetime and seldom, if ever, come in contact with the nightmare monsters that inhabit the caves and cliffs of the ocean floor."

Fire In The Galley Stove
William Outersonx

CHAPTER 1

The night ocean had suddenly come alive.

Ned had never seen anything like it. Beneath the surface, flashing neon lights darted back and forth – *hundreds* of them.

He had run this same night route many times before, but this was something new. Whatever they were, he could hear the impact as they thumped against the hull of their little cabin cruiser.

"Hey, Wade," Ned called over his shoulder. "Are you seeing this?

Behind him, looking down from the helm, the pilot nodded.

"Red devils," he said. "Jumbo squid. Humboldts. They do that when they're feeding."

"It looks like a laser light-show."

Wade smiled. "Bio-luminescence, they call it."

"I've never seen it."

"They show up from time to time. Sort of like locusts. They chase the shoals of bait-fish."

As Ned looked, he could now see the silvery flashes of what looked like blue-fish, their own slender bodies reflecting among the red flashes of the predators.

"There are a *lot* of them."

"Humboldt squid travel in packs," Wade agreed. "What you see here at the surface is probably only a fraction of what's actually down there." He shook his head. "And trust me, you do *not* want to fall in."

Ned pushed away from the railing. There was no doubt there.

These night jaunts always made him nervous, but he knew it was a necessity. Some deliveries simply couldn't be made by the light of day. And their current cargo could easily earn them ten years in prison.

Of course, if they were capped by the Coast Guard, jail-time would be the least of their problems.

Ned didn't know the exact dollar amount of the packs of white powder smuggled away in their hold, but he knew it was many times more than the value of his life.

Mr. Mason didn't 'fire' his employees. That left loose ends.

Wade, who had been on the job for ten years, had once commented to Ned that working for Colin Mason was a bit like getting married – it was a union meant to last for life.

And 'till death do you part.

Still, it was a fairly straight-forward job. Simple cargo delivery.

Truth to tell, Ned always felt safe enough from the Coast Guard. He frankly doubted there were all that many cops who wanted to run afoul of Colin Mason. Over the years, there had only been a few who tried.

None that were currently still with us.

Looking at it that way, these night deliveries were almost a courtesy to law-enforcement, saving them the risk of being put in harm's way.

For Ned's part, his view on the matter was that they were simply feeding the market – giving the people what they wanted. When push came to shove, all Colin Mason was selling was entertainment. It was no different than the liquor industry. And because the product was in demand, it all was going to happen anyway.

In Ned's mind, 'crime' meant 'theft'. This was simply business. 'Illicit' simply meant the government hadn't taken a big enough cut.

As far as Ned was concerned, *that* was the real theft.

Not that he felt the need to over-justify. He knew his place in the scheme of things well enough. He was a delivery-boy. His job was to get the wares to market.

All he had to do was make sure it *got* there.

Because that was the other part of illicit – it meant the consequences for failure-to-deliver were a little more severe.

Ned looked towards shore. The southern California coast was still several miles out.

For whatever reason, he was feeling edgy tonight, and he wanted this job done.

Below, he could hear the steady thumping as the boat plowed through the swarm of heavy, four and five-foot bodies.

There was also the sound of chopping meat as the things ran through the propeller.

"Jesus," Ned said. "The water's thick with them."

Then there came a heavier thud, and this time the boat lurched in the water.

There was the sound of a struggling engine as the motor sputtered to a stop.

"What the hell was that?" Ned asked.

Wade tried the ignition but got nothing. Frowning, he looked over the side.

"I think something got caught in the propeller."

Wade put the boat into neutral and the two men looked over the stern, peering into the dark water.

All they could see was a large mass under the surface – an indistinct dark shape roughly four-feet wide, clinging to the boat's motor.

"What the hell?" Ned said.

Wade pulled a boat hook from its moorings and reached over the side, poking at the obstruction. But as he did so, the pole itself was suddenly stuck firm as well, as if something had grabbed it from below. Wade pulled at the boat-hook but it wouldn't budge.

Now the dark mass began to glow, flashing like a strobe light, blinking white and then turning red.

Ned felt the first touch of disquiet.

A moment later, a tentacle reached over the railing, just above the motor.

"Jesus!" Ned blurted, stepping back quickly.

The single arm was nearly as big around as his leg. And in place of circular suckers, it was lined with what looked like vicious hooks. There was the sound of scraping wood as the sharp rows of talons dug into the railing.

"What the hell is *that*?" Ned said breathlessly.

"Well, I'll be..." Wade muttered as he moved cautiously to the back of the boat, where the tentacle had latched on, and he shined a light over the railing. Then he turned on the underwater boat lights, illuminating the water beneath them.

The moment he did so, there was another heavy impact as a second massive shape rocketed-up from below. The boat jolted in the water.

"Is that another one?" Ned asked nervously, looking around at the suddenly luminescent water around them.

They could see the ocean full of swarming red devils, their five-foot bodies flashing like emergency lights.

But among them, they could now see larger shapes cruising past. As one passed near the underwater lights, Ned could clearly make out the shape of what looked like a much bigger squid.

"Now *that's* something I've never seen," Wade said.

"They're eating the little ones," Ned said.

"Squid are cannibals," Wade replied.

Suddenly, there were two more heavy blows against the hull, and several of the underwater boat-lights were knocked out.

"Holy *shit*," Wade said, as the boat suddenly lurched heavily in the water. The two men briefly staggered for balance. Ned grabbed the railing.

They felt another heavy thud, this one coming from the stern.

"Are they trying to sink us?" he asked, wide-eyed.

"I don't think so," Wade said, moving to the back of the boat, peering over the railing.

As he looked over the side, they could now see that the first of the things – the one that had latched onto the motor – had been grabbed by two others, and they appeared to be eating it alive. The thing flashed bright red, just like the smaller Humboldts, squirting a billowing cloud of black ink, as it struggled against its fellows.

Stepping away from the railing, Wade shut off the boat lights.

For a moment, the two men blinked in the sudden darkness. But in the water, the glowing shapes stood out as brightly as ever.

As they watched, the beast that had clamped onto the motor suddenly let go. The tentacle latched over the railing released and pulled back over the side.

Ned ran his hand over the rail and the divots in the wood felt like they had been dug by bear claws. He could fit his finger fully inside the groove.

The heavy mass fell away, and they could see the flashing light pulsing from its body as it dropped back below the surface, even as the others continued to eat the thing alive.

It did not, however, let go of the motor. The casing had been torn loose from its mooring, and as the beast pulled away, the motor went with it.

"Ummm," Wade muttered, "that's not good."

Ned looked at him wide-eyed.

"Are we stuck?"

Wade nodded. "Without a motor? Yeah, we're stuck."

They looked around at the surrounding ocean.

The swarm of red devils hadn't slowed, their blinking lights flashed below the surface as they preyed on the schooling bait-fish, even as their larger cousins preyed upon them in turn.

Ned looked at the shore, still several miles distant.

Wade pulled out his phone.

"I'm calling Mr. Mason," he said.

Ned frowned. Mr. Mason didn't like problems. It was also dead in the middle of the night.

But when Wade rang the number, Mason picked up right away, as if waiting by the phone. His voice was typically calm, deceptively easy. But Ned could hear the icy steel underneath.

"This better be good," Mason said.

"Hey, boss," Wade said, "we seem to have run into an unexpected wrinkle."

Wade explained briefly and was greeted by a prolonged silence.

"Well," Mason said finally, "that's a new one for me. Can you fix the motor?"

"It's *gone*, sir," Wade replied.

"Where are you?"

"About seven miles out. Should I put out a GPS signal?"

"No," Mason said sternly. "I don't want the Coast Guard picking up anything. I'll send out a chopper. Once we're in the area, I'll have them call you. We can track you down from there."

"Thank you, sir."

"More importantly," Mason said, "is the cargo secured?"

Wade nodded as if Mason were sitting right in front of him.

"Yes, sir. Down in the hold."

"That's our priority," Mason said. "Keep that firmly in mind."

"Yes, sir," Wade replied and Mason hung up.

Wade pocketed his phone, shrugging to Ned.

"I guess we wait," he said.

Ned glanced unhappily over the side, wondering how long that might be. He took solace knowing Mason wasn't the type to dawdle.

But as he looked over the railing, he realized the water was a lot closer than it had been only a few minutes ago.

"Oh Jesus," he said, "are we sinking?"

Frowning, Wade joined him at the railing, looking over the stern where the motor had been torn away. When he looked back, his pale expression was answer enough.

"I think we're in trouble," he said.

Wade shined his light over the edge at the schooling red devils and the massive shapes darting around them like circling sharks.

As he did so, there was yet another impact against the hull.

"Shut off that light," Ned whispered.

In sudden realization, Wade nodded, blinking the flashlight off.

But the creature had already latched on and now the boat was beginning to tip.

"Get the raft," Wade said breathlessly, even as he reached for his phone.

Ned pulled the square yellow pack from where it was strapped just under the railing.

He looked out at the night ocean, unable to believe it.

Was this really happening?

Mason's voice sounded on Wade's speaker.

"Talk to me."

"Mr. Mason?" Wade said into the phone. "Sir, it's gotten worse. We're sinking."

There was a muttered curse over the speaker.

"Okay," Mason said, his voice a cut-your-losses cool, "then set the GPS. We need to mark that cargo."

"We're sinking fast, sir," Wade said.

"Then you better hurry," Mason replied.

Wade glanced at Ned. They both knew better than to let Mason down on this one.

"Yes, sir," Wade said.

"The chopper's on its way," Mason assured. "Hang on."

The connection blinked off.

Wade climbed up to the pilot's station, and activated the GPS device bolted under the radio.

Ned pulled the chord on the inflatable raft, tossing it over the side. There was a blast of air as the rubber raft inflated automatically. He could see the darting shapes, blinking under the surface.

The water was already filling over the stern as the two men climbed into the lifeboat.

Then there was a flash of electric light and a smell of ozone as the boat's power went out. The lights blinked off and left them sitting in darkness.

Wade pushed away from the sinking wreck.

Ned couldn't even see his face in the dark.

But they could still see the light-show below.

As the boat slid beneath the surface, the two men sat in silence.

Then there was a splash as a tentacle reached over the side of the raft and latched onto Wade's shoulder.

"Oh, *shit*...," he blurted, a half-second before he was snatched and pulled into the water.

"*Wade!*"

Ned moved reflexively to grab for him but Wade was already gone.

Below the surface, Ned could see the massive shapes converging, mobbing, blinking strobe-light images of the struggle as they pulled Wade down deep and out of sight.

Ned sat wide-eyed in the dark, afraid to move.

Beneath him, the rubber raft bumped and jostled as the Humboldts contained to swarm.

Jesus, Ned thought, am I going to die tonight?

Helpless, he waited, watching the freeway of lights pass below.

The minutes ticked-off. He had no idea how long, but it seemed like forever.

Mason said he was on his way, but how would they find him in the dark?

And if they did, would he be blamed?

Wade was the pilot, but Ned knew Mason was prone to vent – and the stories of what happened then...?

Well, suffice to say they fit the profile of urban-legend.

Ned shut his eyes, huddling on the little rubber raft as it was buffeted from below, but for the moment, at least, the lifeboat was being ignored.

Then he heard the drone of rotor blades.

When he opened his eyes, Ned saw the approaching light in the sky.

In his pocket, his own phone buzzed.

His hands trembling, Ned reached for his pocket, nearly dropping his phone as he tapped the screen.

Mason's voice sounded over the speaker.

"Ned? I tried to call Wade. He's not answering."

Ned's voice was dry.

"He's gone, sir." He tried not to sound weepy. "The boat's gone down. Those *things*... they took him."

"Hang on," Mason said, "We're coming to get you."

Ned looked up. Mason himself had apparently come along for the ride.

That was another thing – Mason liked to handle his business personally.

The chopper circled, moving in his direction.

Ned waved, even though he knew he was still invisible in the dark.

At least, he was until the spotlight shone down, spearing the raft in a circle of light.

Ned realized what was happening a second too late.

"Mr. Mason, wait..." he began, but then there was a blast of exploding air as the rubber pontoons were slashed and burst.

It wasn't even one of the big ones, Ned saw – the little red devils had latched onto the life-raft as it sat centered in the circle of light.

Water flooded in over the side, and in seconds, he was swimming among them.

Ned had time for one scream before the Humboldts were upon him, red lights flashing like an ambulance, but the siren was in his own head.

They mobbed. Ned felt the sting of sawed suckers and biting beaks. And as he was pulled down, he saw the first of the larger shapes circling towards him.

It was a moment of cruelty when he realized he was going to die after all.

He could still see the spotlight on the surface above, as he was dragged down into the depths.

The chopper circled over the empty water. All that remained was the tattered rubber life-raft, still floating, tossing among the waves.

The freeway of lights paraded-on as the red devils continued to feed.

In the chopper above, Colin Mason nodded to his pilot.

"Mark the location," he said.

Then the chopper circled and headed back to shore.

CHAPTER 2

Up from the depths, the submersible slowly rose out of the gloom into the morning light.

Travis Prescott had been a former special-ops combat diver, and he only wished he'd had something like this to play with back in the day. A recent acquisition, donated by a marine conservation foundation, the craft was a clear, spherical bubble, made of a pressure-resistant acrylic sapphire, and fitted with a waldo-operated arm that he could use with a dexterity nearly equal to that of his own fingers.

Currently, the hand-claw was gripped around a six-foot chunk of whale blubber that he had retrieved from more than fifteen-hundred-feet down.

It was a retrieval that had not been without some resistance, because the piece of carrion was somebody's lunch, and the scavengers were not quite ready to give it up.

Dosidicus gigas, the Humboldt squid – *diablo rojo,* or 'red devil', as the fishermen down in Mexico called them – small but feisty creatures who lived up to the name. Currently, nearly a dozen of them circled his craft, occasionally darting in to latch onto the chunk of purloined blubber, frantically tearing away pieces, as if starving.

When he had stumbled onto the piece of carrion down below, it had been crawling with Humboldts.

Travis was well-acquainted with these pugnacious underwater predators. They fed in large schools, often numbering in the hundreds, and he knew they were not to be underestimated.

Even now, as he approached the surface, they continued to circle his high-tech bubble-craft, their arrow-shaped bodies zooming in, often pausing to look at this strange creature hiding in plain sight, encased in a clear bubble, before racing off again.

Humboldts were actually quite curious and intelligent animals, and they could seem peaceful and serene when they weren't feeding – deceptively so, because they could change their temperament in an instant. Sometimes it was in response to the scent of food, or even a signal of light – bio-luminescence was a common trait among deep-sea animals, and Humboldts, along with most other squid, used it as a form of language and communication.

But never mistake – there was only one reason why they might be checking you out, and that was to ascertain whether you were something they wanted to eat. Travis' own arms and torso bore the scars of not recognizing the difference until it was nearly too late.

Sometimes they would move on you because you acted like prey. And sometimes, it was just because they'd taken stock and decided they had enough numbers to take you down.

Travis had actually hesitated before moving in with the submersible. The chunk of blubber seemed to move like a thing alive, as it was tugged and ripped by the circling Humboldts. Red devils were known to mob targets, and if enough of them battened down, it was possible their sheer weight could hold him down here, or potentially even incapacitate the sub.

It was the sort of thing that had happened before. Humboldt squid were known to behave aggressively towards unfamiliar objects in their territory, attacking deep-water cameras and remote drones, rendering them inoperable.

Taking an aggressive stance of his own, Travis moved in with bright flashing lights. In the past, it had worked to scatter them.

Not always. Sometimes, it actually seemed to draw them in.

But this time, as he reached for the chunk of blubber with the automated claw, the squid gave ground, flashing their own bio-luminescent outrage at the intrusion on their meal, skirting around in wide circles, sometimes passing in close, their bodies blinking bright red, as they went darting past.

Travis thought that was going to be the extent of it until the first of them suddenly latched onto the automated arm, apparently ready to make a fight of it. Seconds later, half-a-dozen more battened down on the submersible itself. Travis could see the suckers, attempting to get a grip on the transparent alloy casing, the hooks on their two longest tentacles struggling to latch on.

The submersible's ascent was slowed alarmingly by their added weight, but Travis had seen this behavior before, and was ready for it. He pushed a button on his console and there was the sudden blue flash of an electric charge transmitted through the water.

Instantly, the Humboldts released and scattered in a flock.

They did not, however, retreat, and continued hovering, albeit at a respectful distance. Several of them remained on his tail all the way to the surface and remained circling below.

The boat waiting above was another donation, outfitted with equipment nearly as sophisticated as the sub itself.

After he'd left the military, Travis had founded an underwater exploration society, taking his passion for diving into the private sector, and he'd produced several documentaries focusing on deep-sea fauna, and squid in particular.

Travis had become something of a celebrity-expert on the subject, although the true scholar was the man who waited in the tricked-out vessel above.

Professor Clyde Spencer was considered the world's foremost expert on squid, and he had partnered with Travis for the last ten years.

The professor was standing, leaning over the railing, waving as Travis brought the submersible up beside the modest-sized little schooner.

At seventy-five, Clyde had spent a lifetime on the water, which had left him spry and whipcord fit, although at his age, he still left most of the physical duties to Travis, while monitoring their deep-water discoveries via video from the boat.

Currently, he was holding his nose as Travis brought the piece of rotting whale fat to the surface.

"Whew!" Clyde said, as Travis popped the hatch on the submersible. "That's awful."

Travis pulled himself out of the high-tech bubble.

"They didn't want to give it up, either. They're still down there."

Even as he said it, there were flashes of light in the water, just at the edge of their field of vision.

Clyde smiled. "I expect so."

He reached over with a gaff and pulled the floating chunk of blubber in close.

As if the movement acted as a trigger, or possibly mimicked the vibrations of struggling prey, several of the circling squid became emboldened, darting up to latch onto the smelly mound of blubber, and began tearing away at it once again.

Travis looked around at the surrounding water. It was well into morning, and the sun had risen prominently into the sky. You usually didn't see the Humboldts at the surface during the day. While they were actually fairly common in these waters, they typically didn't show up until dusk, chasing the schools of bait-fish as they rose up to feed.

But the red devils were thick this year.

Travis had first encountered them during a dive way back in 2002 – another boom population year where these 'jumbo squid' had swarmed the local coast like locusts.

It had been his first year out of the service and Travis had been traveling the world. And on this particular occasion, he was diving in the Sea of Cortes – not far south of the California border, and a known hot-spot for Humboldt squid.

He had hired an area fisherman to take him and his camera out to where the red devils were congregating, despite the warnings from the locals.

As Travis had dressed down into his scuba gear, the fisherman who'd brought him had shaken his head, his expression somewhere between bemusement and disbelief, and told him in broken English, "Okay, you go down, you gonna die."

Travis, of course, had not been afraid. He'd spent his life training divers to keep their heads underwater. He'd performed more than two-hundred live-combat operations in hostile waters. He had also dived with all the most notorious marine predators, including Great White and tiger sharks. Once, he had even dived overboard into the middle of a pod of orcas attacking a full-grown sperm whale.

In Travis' experience, animals were only dangerous if you were stupid.

On this particular occasion, that axiom had come back to bite him – quite literally.

He had dropped over the side of the boat into the school of Humboldts, just letting himself drift as they initially gave ground, circling around him.

The squid had only just risen to the surface for their nightly feeding, and their bio-luminescence flashed in pulsing steady strobes as the bait-fish schooled around them, the passage of their bodies rippling the water like wind.

It was actually rather calming.

After their initial shyness, the Humboldts had come in closer to investigate.

Travis was fascinated. He was struck by how beautiful these ungainly alien creatures appeared in their home environment. They moved as gracefully as any sea-creature he had ever seen – stopping on a dime, their heads perked behind their arms and tentacles, only to go darting off, disappearing in an instant into the surrounding blue.

Presently, one of them had come right up to him and his camera.

The big eyes seemed to regard him with real intelligence. The little creature pulsed with biological light. Always fascinated by such wonders, Travis found himself rapt.

Or perhaps *lulled*, might be a better word – because he didn't see several other squid circling around, approaching from the rear.

Then suddenly he was grabbed from behind. There was a sharp pain in his shoulders and neck as tentacles wrapped around him and he felt the dig of a chomping beak the size of a pinball.

Before he knew it, he was surrounded. His arms and legs were seized and he felt the sawed-suckers sinking into his flesh as the beaks bit through his wet-suit and began carving chunks out of him.

He was also being dragged down deep.

Within moments, he was pulled down into the dark.

He realized then, that if he didn't fight back, he was about to die.

In a surge of motion, he began punching and kicking at his attackers. One of them had latched onto his wrist, and he felt the bone snap.

Travis weighed-in at a solid two-hundred and twenty pounds of combat-trained muscle, but these little forty and fifty-pound beasts attacked with a ferocity that he had not been expecting, and it was a sustained assault he had never seen in a wild animal before.

He was dragged nearly seventy-feet down, before he started to fight back in earnest, battling his way loose and swimming for the surface.

Undaunted, the red devils had followed, grabbing at his legs.

He kicked loose, losing both his swim-fins, and was actually forced to stop and throw punches as they attempted to latch onto him once again.

They were still on his tail when he made the surface, bloodied and with a broken wrist, signaling for the boat.

The old fisherman spotted him and had moved quickly, obviously expecting trouble, otherwise it might not have been over yet – the circling shapes had made one last run at him as he hauled himself out of the water.

His camera had taken damage as well, losing its lens and part of its casing, but the footage survived and became the centerpiece of his first documentary. It had also attracted the attention of Professor Spencer, and ignited a decades-long interest.

Fifteen years in the Special Forces and Travis had never gotten a scratch on him, but five minutes diving with Humboldt squid had left him with divots across his chest and shoulders like shrapnel – beak-shaped scars that could hold water.

That had been in the Sea of Cortes. In the intervening years, the population of red devils had spread far and wide, all the way up into Alaska. They seemed to invade new territories, swarming by the thousands, only to disappear weeks later.

By all indications, this was going to be another boom year.

The coast of southern California was always Humboldt habitat, but now there were more of them than ever.

According to Clyde, there were a number of very good reasons for that.

Several events this year had contributed to the conditions for this particular invasion.

Perhaps most significantly, earlier this season, there had been unusual instances of orca predation along the coast. When orcas came to town, other animals panicked. White sharks were well-known to abandon long-established hunting grounds, and there had also been mass beachings of several pods of whales.

Nothing in nature operates in a vacuum, and every action has consequence. The absence of the big baleen whales meant more bait-fish – no pods of giant mouths scooping up whole schools of sardines and herring, their throats billowed out like bullfrogs as they gulped them down. That meant more food for the squid.

Then there were at least two pods of sperm whales that had been lost, both to beachings and orcas, and the big cachalots were the primary predator of the larger squid species.

A longer-term factor was over-fishing of competing predators like sharks, as well as other predatory fish like tuna.

It was a perfect storm – squid reproduce in high numbers, but also usually experience an extremely high mortality, with probably less than two percent surviving to reach adulthood. The absence of predators meant higher survival rates.

There was also a secondary consequence of all those whale beachings that might have contributed locally, as exemplified by the chunk of whale blubber Travis had retrieved from the depths just today.

All those dead whales had been towed offshore, but because of the presence of orcas, there were no white sharks to eat the carcasses.

It was an enormous amount of food, and that meant fat, well-fed Humboldts.

And apparently not just Humboldts, either. This year, it seemed the jumbo squid had been joined by their larger cousins.

As the chunk of blubber bumped against the hull of the boat, Clyde leaned over to inspect the beak marks.

"These," he said, indicating a cup-shaped bite the size of a soccer-ball, "are not the work of a red devil."

Travis had seen those as well. And he knew what they were.

"That," Clyde said, "came from a Colossal."

DEVILFISH

CHAPTER 3

The Colossal squid was the largest invertebrate in the ocean.

Clyde reached down, measuring the bite marks on the blubber.

"That's big," he said, "but they get bigger than that."

Travis nodded respectfully. Clyde's own attack story was a good deal more horrific than his own.

Colossal squid were relatively new on the map of public knowledge, but history had recorded numerous encounters over the centuries – incidents that had been traditionally tossed off as either fish-tales and rumor, or attributed to their cousins, the giant squid – long regarded as the 'Kraken' of myth.

Travis, however, suspected that it was the Colossal squid that was the true Kraken. It was the difference between talons and suckers, and a few hundred pounds versus weights upwards of a ton, not to mention that soccer-ball-sized beak.

There was also the matter of temperament, which was a factor that couldn't be overstated.

The giant squid was actually relatively common in most oceans. Its reclusive nature reflected the fact that it lived down deep, and unlike the smaller Humboldts, it did not often rise to the surface. Nevertheless, carcasses had been washing up on beaches for hundreds of years – sometimes even appearing in large numbers.

Colossal squid, on the other hand, populated the southern oceans surrounding Antarctica, thriving in an environment that was as inhospitable to humans on the geographical surface up top as the deep depths in which they dwelled. There was also limited land mass available for their dead carcasses to wash ashore.

They were not unknown to science – beaks had been found in the bellies of sperm whales – *much* larger than even a giant squid – and the hides of cachalots often exhibited long,

18

dragging, tiger-like claw-marks, that were very different from the saw-edged suckers that lined the arms of giant squid.

In recent years, however, more of them had started to surface.

It was Clyde's theory that Colossals experienced population booms, just like the red devils, although on a much wider scale – perhaps separated by multiple decades or even centuries.

He also believed these population cycles caused their range to periodically expand, branching out much further north.

In fact, Clyde maintained there was at least one fatal incident involving a Colossal squid in the waters just south of the California border, and that the victim was his own father.

"We had a little vacation house near the ocean," Clyde had told Travis, "and he liked to take me and my sister out on the bay. It was a nice little area, cut-off from the main ocean, so the water wasn't too rough, but it still brought in some of the more exotic sea-life that you saw in the tropics. And one summer, there was an invasion of red devils. He was eager to go out and see."

Travis had heard many versions of this same story involving Humboldt squid, which wasn't all that different from his own. People often thought of the ocean as recreation, and treated natural events like a fireworks display for their amusement. And admittedly, his own first-time tryst with Humboldts reflected a similar arrogance – one that had nearly cost him his life.

Clyde's father hadn't been as lucky.

"We had brought along our fishing rods," Clyde said, "and once we saw them swarming, my father put out a line in the water."

Again, this was a common element Travis had heard before – a small boat and fishing line.

"He hadn't even secured the rod when the line was hit."

Clyde shook his head.

"I remember him laughing as he stood up in the boat, bracing against the tug on the line. And a second later, he was pulled over."

Clyde had been eight years old at the time, his sister ten. Watching from the boat, they had watched as their father was set-upon by the swarming Humboldts.

"My sister gunned the motor," Clyde said, "and we made our way over to where he was struggling in the water. We could see them clinging to him, and he was *screaming*. I had never heard my father *scream* before."

Travis remembered well those digging claws and biting beaks, and the dotted scars all over his own arms and legs.

"But he was a strong swimmer," Clyde said, "and he managed to fight his way back to our boat. I remember grabbing his hand. He actually started to laugh as he pulled himself back on board, trying to reassure us that everything was going to be alright. With blood running down his face.

"But then something bigger grabbed him."

Clyde always told the story the same way, in the same verbiage, as if compartmentalizing it away in his own mind.

"I saw a tentacle the size of my leg lash across his face. And it had *claws*."

He was always adamant on that point. "*Claws*. Not suckers."

Clyde shrugged. "It pulled him down, and we never saw him again."

This would have been long before the days of cell-phones. Clyde's ten-year-old sister had finally steered the little outboard back to the dock and they had called the police.

Their father's body was never found, so there had never been an autopsy. The kids' story was taken with a grain of salt by the authorities – a 'giant' squid to a ten and an eight-year old didn't have to be very big, and it was generally assumed that he had simply been taken by the Humboldts.

But Clyde knew what he saw. And Travis suspected at least part of Clyde's life-long obsession was to prove what had happened was real.

"We were out on the water for hours," Clyde said. "I could see the bigger squid under the water, chasing the red devils. They were eating them."

That had been less than a hundred miles south.

And now, as Travis tied the six-foot chunk of squid-ravaged whale blubber to the side of their boat, Clyde nodded as if in affirmation.

He snapped several pictures of the large scoops taken out of the smelly rotting flesh, making sure to include the smaller bite marks left by the Humboldts.

"They're back," he said.

CHAPTER 4

Ashley was already up and on her way to the beach when she got the call that human bodies had washed ashore.

She was the youngest on-camera field reporter for the local network news station, and a recent hire. And only a few years out of college, she was full of ambition.

Ashley's interest, however, had never been so much journalism as getting into broadcasting – her on-the-ground anchorette position was a related field, which she hoped would lead into something more congenial.

Being called by her producer first thing in the morning to go look at dead bodies was not what she had signed-up for.

She hoped it wasn't too grody. She *hated* those. Bodies lost at sea got nibbled at by any number of critters, and when you found them, they were always crawling with crabs and worms. The first time she'd been sent out to report on a simple drowning, one look at the bulging dead eyes staring up from the pale, fish-white face had caused her to turn around and puke.

The local Coast Guard officer still gave her a hard time over that one.

Ashley had a sun-and-surf day planned – a working holiday.

Beach City was one of the southern-most resort burgs that dotted the California coast, and the town hosted a yearly surf contest. This year, Ashley had drawn hosting honors. In anticipation of her on-camera bikini appearance, she had aerobicized mercilessly for the better part of two-weeks, and she was looking *primed*.

An early-morning viewing of bloated corpses was not the way she wanted to start out the day.

It had already been an oddball year for the communities that lived off the ocean, most of whom depended upon tourism.

For one thing, there had been a lot of shark activity earlier in the season – not unusual in California, especially in recent years, because the migrating seal colonies made the area a hot-spot for Great Whites. There were areas further up the coast where the surf-industry was suffering for it. In fact, one small burg had seen repeated attacks off the same beach for a period of years.

But this year, the white sharks had vacated their hunting grounds early, after a high-profile invasion of killer whales. Ashley herself had run a brief piece on the subject just last week – ostensibly for public interest, but more truthfully to allay public concerns over any lingering Great Whites in the days before Beach City's single-biggest yearly tourism draw.

In point of fact, the Surf Shore attacks had most likely bumped this year's numbers, as beach-goers migrated down south to supposedly safer waters.

Ashley hoped a couple of bodies washed ashore wouldn't derail the event. She also hoped it wasn't a shark attack, although it *had* occurred to her that any Great Whites fleeing Surf Shore might conceivably pass through Beach City on their way out of town.

On the other hand, the absence of sharks was most likely the reason the bodies had made it to shore at all.

She had been driving along the beach and now she spotted the emergency vehicles parked just at the edge of a little cove – a little mini-peninsula that tended to catch ocean debris and trash from the public beaches. Today, it had washed up something a little more ominous.

The Coast Guard officer saw her car and waved her down.

Lieutenant Randy Collins operated the one-man guard-post just south of Beach City, which was just about the last stop before the Mexican border, and he had been the officer on hand when Ashley had puked-up her guts at the sight of her first half-decomposed cadaver.

There was also an ambulance on-site, along with the coroner's van and the local police chief.

They all waved as Ashley parked her car and stepped out.

Collins smiled as she came walking up.

"I hope you haven't eaten yet," he said.

Ashley looked down to where two plastic tarps had been laid out, covering a pair of rather minimal-looking bundles still lying on the beach. She wasn't encouraged that the paramedic standing over them appeared a little bit green himself.

The police chief, an older guy named Mathews, had shaken his head.

"This is a bad one," he said.

Terrific. She knew they couldn't wait for her to get a look.

"What happened?" Ashley asked.

The coroner shrugged. He was a non-local, who Ashley hadn't met before. He introduced himself as Everett, as he turned to the innocuous-looking tarps lying discreetly on the sand.

"Well," he said, "I can't tell you that for sure, but a picture paints a thousand words."

Everett nodded to the paramedic who pulled away the first tarp.

Ashley had prepared herself for something bad.

It wasn't nearly enough.

Without formality, she turned and threw-up her morning coffee and donuts.

There was a murmur of laughter from the men as she gagged onto the sand.

Great, she thought, as her eyes watered, ruining her carefully-applied, supposedly waterproof mascara that she had donned just for the day.

"What," she managed, "did *that*?"

"Well," Mathews said, "it ain't a shark. That's for sure."

The body under the tarp was nearly skeletonized. The tissue had been gnawed away nearly to the bone. There was barely enough decomposing meat for the crabs and squirming worms.

Ashley felt another pulse of nausea.

Collins pulled the tarp back discreetly, covering the body.

"Not a shark," he agreed. "Honestly, it looks more like a piranha."

Ashley shut her eyes, but the visual remained burned like an after-image.

"Actually," Everett said, "I've seen wounds like this before. It looks to me like it was a squid."

"A squid?" Ashley responded. "You mean like, 'release the Kraken'?"

Everett smiled.

"Something like that."

Ashley shook her head.

"We've got a major beach event going on today. And you're telling me people are being killed by squid?"

"I didn't say killed," Everett replied. "My guess is that this was a boat accident. Whatever ate these guys was probably just scavenging after the victims drowned."

Collins frowned.

"There was no distress signal sent out in the last twenty-four hours."

Behind them, Chief Mathews' phone beeped. He checked his message. Then he looked up at the others.

"I just might have an explanation for that. You'll never guess who's been in contact with the mayor." Mathews eyed them meaningfully. "Colin Mason."

"No kidding," Collins said.

"Who's Colin Mason?" Ashley asked.

Collins smiled sardonically.

"And you're in the news business." He shook his head. "Colin Mason is no one you want to know."

Collins nodded to Chief Mathews.

"I'll get out on the water and see what I can find. My guess is there's a shipment of something very expensive and very illegal within a day's float."

Collins turned to Everett.

"Why don't you get hold of the Oceanographic Institute up north. Send them some pictures and see what they've got to say." Collins indicated the covered tarps. "The mayor's going to want to know if there's any risk going forward with the Surf Rally today."

Everett was shaking his head.

"Most of these wounds seem postmortem. There's so much tissue missing, it's hard to tell for sure, but I frankly doubt there's any danger." He shrugged. "At least no more than there always is in the ocean. Certainly, no more risk than a bunch of daredevils riding waves. The reef is probably a bigger hazard than the wildlife."

Everett nodded confidently.

"In all honesty, I'd say this is simply a case of scavengers consuming carrion."

Collins eyed him seriously.

"And I expect you to get on the horn to the Institute and get someone *there* to say that."

Everett nodded. "Understood."

Collins smiled at Ashley.

"I think your Surf Rally is safe," he said, "but we're going to play it smart."

Ashley nodded. She was due at the beach in an hour.

"I'll scout out the coast, and get in touch with you after I've talked to the mayor."

Collins smiled.

"In the meantime," he said, "you might want to fix your make-up. Maybe a breath-mint."

Ashley smiled ruefully, tasting the left over bile on her lips.

She turned back to her car as the paramedic pulled out a stretcher and prepared to load the bodies aboard the ambulance. She tapped a brief text-message to her producer.

As she drove away, she caught her face in the mirror, frowning at the mess of her carefully-prepared make-up.

She turned toward the public beaches, but found she was no longer looking forward to the event.

The zest had gone out of the day.

CHAPTER 5

If Ashley had been concerned rumors of dead bodies might hurt the event, it turned out, she needn't have worried.

When she got to the beach, the high-adrenaline crowd was already talking about it animatedly. And once she started interviewing contestants, they couldn't wait to share their own near-miss encounters – everything from shark attacks to high-velocity impacts with jagged rocks. Her first twenty-minutes of interview-footage was a series of one-up stories of near-death experiences, all told with the jovial air of relating fondly-remembered good-times.

Last year's champion was a walrus-sized fellow called Tank – boisterous and barrel-shaped, a far-cry from the ripped torsos of most of the strapping young studs, you would never guess he was an athlete.

Tank had actually been the target of a live, on-camera attack by a Great White, only a few years before. It had been a relatively minor incident, where the shark had sidled up to him sitting on his board and had taken a bite right out of it, missing his leg by barely six inches.

A loud, "Holy shit!" had sounded over the air, as Tank had scrambled and was pulled clear of the water by one of the gathered fan-boats. Today, he related that story to Ashley with gusty laughter.

Another of this year's favorites, a first-timer at the Beach City contest, named Rudy – shaved clean and tattooed from head-to-toe – told the tale and displayed the scar of a barracuda attack – a ten-inch slash across the thigh.

While Ashley was glad the contestants were in good-spirits, the stories had cranked-up her own anxiety-levels. The network had set her up with her own paddle-board this year, and she stood balanced out on the water, with her boat's camera's on her, as she narrated.

She found herself looking uncomfortably at the surrounding water. Right at the edge of the reef, just before the waves began to break, the churning current made it impossible to see the bottom.

In the interest of responsibility, Lieutenant Collins had called the mayor – a hypochondriac little man, named Vernon, who Ashley had worried might simply up and cancel the entire event.

Again, Ashley needn't have worried. The surf contest was Beach City's primary revenue generator for the entire year, and hypochondriac or not, Vernon was looking for assurances first.

They had not yet heard back from the Oceanographic Institute, but Collins had repeated the coroner's summation, including the part about how every time you went into the ocean, you entered a wilderness full of more dangerous predators than you would ever want to know.

Mayor Vernon had not looked particularly reassured, but he had allowed the event to go on.

Still, the hypochondriac in him showed when Ashley interviewed him for his public statement.

Vernon had been shown pictures of the bodies, and combined with the stories circulating across the beach about every other near-fatal encounter in the world, the mayor appeared more than a little pale.

And just because she had a little bit of orneriness in her and couldn't resist it, Ashley had asked him about the two corpses that had washed ashore.

Vernon had looked unhappily back and forth between her and the camera.

"Well," he said, "I've been assured there is no danger."

Among the more colorful characters making an appearance this year was a young newcomer that Ashley had never seen before, who introduced himself as Brody Wilson.

Ashley was accustomed to getting hit-on during these type of events – in fact, she actually counted on it – her bikini body was one of her on-camera selling points, and consistently attracted all the appropriate attention from the young, wild beach studs, and this year's crop didn't disappoint.

Brody, in particular, seemed to have set his sights on her. Arrogantly handsome and bubbling with the unbridled confidence of invincible youth, he clearly appeared to be enjoying every second of his life.

Ashley envied that sort of thing.

And *oh*, but he was a deadly charmer. Ashley knew the type well – *loved* the type – and she was absolutely, determined never to go anywhere near the type ever again – not since her last bout of Tequila.

Still, she found the attention boosted her spirits, banishing lingering images of cannibalized corpses, and she began to have fun.

They went live at ten, announced with an overture of music from a floating platform right at the edge of the reef. Ashley was perched on her board just short of where the swells began.

There was one last moment of anxiety right before they went on the air – brief visions of sharks rising from the murky depths, targeting surface objects like seals – but then she pushed the thought firmly away, offering the cameras her brightest and most engaging smile.

"Greetings!" she said, tossing her hair with a practiced flourish, "I'm Ashley Wells, and welcome to Beach City!"

The music turned up as the camera panned to the contestants lining up along the breakers, poised for their first runs.

Ashley went through her initial introduction, her producer breaking away with snips of her pre-filmed interviews with each contestant, along with footage of previous years.

And apparently, just to add spice, cuts from all the shark stories, including clips of Tank's own on-camera attack, before cutting back as the surfers began making their first practice runs.

As Brody passed her on his board, he flashed his own sun-and-surf smile.

"How 'bout I buy you dinner tonight?" he called out on-camera. "I've got prize money coming!"

Ashley had smiled despite herself. Turning to the camera, she called out to the live audience.

"What do you think, folks? Have I got a date?"

Standing-up on his board, Brody tipped an imaginary hat, before veering into the first of the cresting waves.

The cameras zoomed back as he went into his run, arrowing right through the curling tunnels of water.

Each surfer had been fitted with a GoPro, and the screen switched back-and-forth from the panoramic view to Brody's own POV as he shot through the wave-tunnel.

Ashley had done her share of surfing, and knew the rush of that moment when you entered the water-pipeline, and well-understood the addiction – it was like flying through hyper-space – 'tubular', they called it.

Brody launched like a rocket through the cresting swell, turning nearly inverted as he began to boogie, twisting his board beneath him like a bucking bronco.

The crowd on the beach and the gathered boats broke into applause as he shot out from the other end of the water tunnel, raising his arms as if already claiming victory.

Ashley's smile was genuine as she turned to the camera.

"It's going to be a good one this year, folks," she said.

Tank was laughing as he moved-in for his own first run.

"Not bad, kid, but don't count your money yet!"

Tank made a bee-line for the rising swells, perching his unlikely physique up on his board like a sprinter waiting for the starting gun.

The water beneath the waves actually seemed to sparkle in the sun.

A moment later, Ashley felt a bump beneath her feet.

When she looked down, she realized that the reflecting shimmer was actually coming from schools of fish flocking just beneath the surface.

That was nothing unusual, and Ashley thought little of it as Tank pulled into the wave and began his first run.

At first, Ashley thought the flash of red-blinking light was coming from one of the cameras on the surrounding boats.

Then something tipped Tank's board, sending him tumbling into the waves.

There was a ripple of laughter murmuring over the gathered crowds as the defending champion was tossed into the surf.

Ashley was smiling as she turned towards the camera. She had been about to say something wry and witty when she again felt her own board bumped from below. She saw another flash of red, this time blinking from the water beneath her feet.

Tank had popped back to the surface, grabbing his board as the wave receded.

He began to scream.

A second later, he was pulled under.

There was a brief moment where the only sound was the music blasting from the speakers on the judge's float.

Ashley paused, steadying herself on her own board, looking cautiously down into the water.

Among the rush of schooling bait-fish, reflecting like silver coins, she now clearly saw larger, four and five-foot shapes moving among them, blinking like traffic lights.

There was no sign of Tank.

Several other contestants, including Rudy and Brody, paddled over to where he'd disappeared.

A moment later, there was another scream as Rudy was knocked into the surf. He rose up a couple of seconds later, grabbing at his board.

It looked like he was covered in strips of seaweed.

Then he was pulled under too.

Suddenly poised and alert, Brody was now standing on his own board, watching the water around him warily.

The other surfers circled, looking for any sign of Rudy, and now the lifeguard boats were moving in.

Ashley's producer was talking in her ear, asking what was happening.

Then the paddle board beneath her feet jostled again and she was thrown into the water.

She felt the bumping passage of schooling fish as she floundered, clambering towards the surface.

In the water, she could see the red-blinking shapes darting all around her.

She realized what was happening a moment before she was grabbed by both legs.

There was a stinging pain, like the lash of a whip, as she felt herself pulled under.

She started to scream but choked on water. She grasped desperately for her board, but it was already out of reach. More of the red-glowing shapes darted past her, chasing after the sprinting bait-fish, but now a couple of them were turning in her direction.

Even as she began to fight, the images of skeletonized corpses flashed through her mind, injecting adrenaline into her system.

But she had sucked water and was already beginning to drown.

She couldn't believe it – it had only been a few seconds.

Now there were flashing lights in her own head as her oxygen-starved brain began to blink from consciousness.

Then she felt herself grabbed again, by the arms this time, and she was jerked towards the surface.

The heavy mass that had latched onto her legs resisted, and suddenly there was someone else in the water beside her.

Clinging to his safety cord, Brody had jumped in and was beating at the creature gripping her leg, poking at the bulbous eyes. There was a squirt of black ink as the creature let go, flashing red as it retreated.

But more of the darting shapes were circling in. Brody yanked his cord, pulling his board in close, hauling them both up on top.

Ashley choked and gagged, throwing up water. She grabbed onto the board in a death-grip, looking down at her bloodied arms and legs, as Brody began paddling them towards shore.

A moment later, they were intercepted by her camera boat, and pulled on-board.

Around them, the Coast Guard boats were pulling remaining contestants from the surf. Several of them were lashed and bloody.

In the water, the feeding frenzy continued, a circling swarm of four and five-foot glowing shapes, cannibalizing the shimmering schools of fish.

There was no sign of Tank or Rudy.

Someone finally thought to turn off the music.

Ashley blinked. Her cameraman was staring back at her wide-eyed. She had no idea what her producer was saying because she'd lost her head-piece.

She turned to Brody.

"You saved my life," she said.

Looking a bit shaken himself, Brody smiled back.

"Hey," he said, "I guess this means dinner's on *you*."

Ashley nodded mutely.

In the background, the music had now been replaced by the sound of emergency sirens.

CHAPTER 6

Brody rode with Ashley to the hospital. In the trauma of the moment, she didn't object as he had simply climbed into the ambulance beside her, offering a comforting hand while the paramedics bandaged her up.

As the ambulance pulled away, they could see the scene of chaos left behind. Emergency vehicles crowded the beach while the medics tended to the injured.

Overhead, news helicopters circled – the major networks were taking over as the story broke.

And out on the water, the feeding frenzy had ended as suddenly as it began. The schooling bait-fish broke ranks, heading back out to sea, and the Humboldts followed.

Tank and Rudy remained missing.

"Hell of a first date," Brody remarked, turning away from the window as the ambulance left the beach behind.

Ashley looked down at her bandaged arms and legs, the white fabric seeping red as her cuts bled through the gauze. She grimaced. The wounds were covered up now, but she had seen the circular marks dug into her smooth, tanned skin.

"Oh God," she said. "It's going to be *hideous*."

Brody smiled reassuringly.

"Just tell people they're tattoos," he said. "Besides, most people are going to be looking at the rest of you, anyway."

Ashley wasn't certain whether to be irritated or flattered. At least two people were dead, no telling how many injured, and he was still flirting.

But under the circumstance, it was hard to hold it against him. She took pertinent note of the untreated sucker marks lining his own arms. She'd known him less than an hour and he'd already bled on her behalf while managing to save her life.

Maybe the cockiness was just how he coped.

"You're lucky, you know," he said. "I've dived with Humboldts, and they can be pretty nasty."

Ashley nodded ruefully. "So I've come to understand."

"Seriously," he said. "They aren't like sharks. Once they move on you, they keep coming. Sharks are actually pretty skittish. And they really aren't interested in us. Humboldts will eat anything. And they're aggressive. They would have dragged you down."

"So why on Earth would you want to dive with them?"

Brody shrugged.

"Why bungee-jump? Why go sky-diving?"

"I have absolutely no idea," Ashley replied. "I like scuba-diving too, but not with sharks."

Brody smiled.

"Honey," he said, "if you've dived in the ocean, then you've dived with sharks. Whether you knew it or not."

He pulled out his phone, tapping his screen awake.

"It's like anything," he said. "It's dangerous to drive a car if you don't understand your perimeters. Humboldts are like any animal. You need to pick your moments if you want to interact with them. And feeding-time is not one of them. Hell, even the family dog can get pretty growly if you get too near their food dish."

Ashley's family dog had been a golden retriever and you could have pried a milk bone out of her mouth and beat her with a club before she showed her teeth.

"Here," Brody said, pulling out his phone. He held up the screen, showing video clips of circling squid. "I took this a couple of years ago, down in Mexico."

Ashley nodded. An adrenaline-junkie then. This was exactly why she avoided guys like Brody, Tequila or no Tequila.

He tapped his phone again, this time bringing up an image of a diver clinging to the fin of a twelve-foot Great White shark.

Ashley shook her head. And she thought *cage*-diving was stupid.

"This is you too?"

Brody smiled. "That was the same trip."

"Do you have a death-wish?"

He shook his head.

"No. A *life*-wish." He held up his own sucker-marked arms. "Never had a scratch on me until today. That's the difference in picking your moments."

He tapped his phone again.

"By the way," he said, "it looks like you're trending."

He held up the screen.

The headline read, 'Sea Monsters Attack Beach', with a sub-text in bold, 'Local Reporter Injured'.

Below was a video of Ashley out on her paddle-board, recording the moments right up until she was knocked into the water.

And below that, there were a series of her publicity pictures – glamour photos and several bikini shots – all part of the portfolio she'd compiled to get her on-camera job.

Brody smiled, as he scrolled down approvingly.

"Any publicity is good publicity," he said.

As he said it, Ashley realized she'd left her own phone, along with her wallet and her purse, back at the beach with her car.

The story was going national. Her producer was probably trying to contact her even now.

Brody was more right than he knew. In journalistic parlance, Ashley realized she had become part of the story.

She looked down at her bandaged arms and now she saw opportunity. She looked up at Brody.

"Can I borrow your phone?" she asked.

CHAPTER 7

Lindsey had known Colin Mason for almost four years, but she had never seen him like this before.

But she knew better than to question – as was her function, she just did what she was told.

Today, that meant stretching herself out on a recliner in the sun, up on the top deck of his yacht, which was anchored just offshore of Beach City, only a few miles up the coast from where today's surf-contest had gotten bloody.

Lindsey had never actually been on Mason's yacht before. Usually, he kept her local. It had been an acceptable arrangement for the last four years, ever since he'd found her dancing at one of the many 'gentleman's clubs' he owned all down the coast. He'd set her up in a ritzy apartment and paid all the bills. All she had to do was be there. And occasionally run the odd errand.

But Mason seemed to want her with him this time – not for company exactly, or even for her feminine charms. It was rather more like a James Bond villain constantly stroking on a furry white cat. He wanted her on-hand. On a leash.

When he'd arrived late last night, he seemed in a sullen mood – non-communicative.

For her part, Lindsey was happy enough to be ignored, just providing her presence.

She actually hadn't really known much about Colin Mason or his family other than what the other girls at the club had told her, but there was no shortage of rumor. When she'd first caught his fancy, the reaction from her co-workers had been a mixture of reverence and awe.

But there had also been a none-too-subtle undercurrent of unease.

If the rumors hadn't been off-putting enough, all that it took was simply to look at him.

For one thing, he was missing his right leg, amputated at the hip. The story was that it had been bitten off by a shark while he had been diving in the Farallon Islands – now known to be a hot-spot for Great Whites.

Mason had been a young man at the time, already carrying a reputation among the more clandestine industries that operated out of California, as a particularly ruthless heir to an already-infamous family name, with ties to both Vegas and Chicago.

Or perhaps '*connections*' would be a better word.

Shark attacks made news wherever they happened, even in the days before the Internet. Mason's attack had actually been caught on film by one of the passengers on his yacht, and the footage – pre-digital VHS camcorder tape – had made its way to the airwaves.

Mason had been recovering in the hospital at the time – a convalescence that had taken months for a full recovery – and the story was that he was none too happy about his misfortune being put into the public domain.

Further rumor was that the individual who had captured the footage had wound-up back at the Farallons himself later that same season. More footage was taken that day as he was thrown to the sharks. It was said Mason kept the tape, labeled on his desk.

Among others. Because it was further rumored that, since then, the Farallon Islands had become one of his favorite dumping grounds. They were more than twenty-miles off the coast of San Francisco and no bodies ever made it to shore.

There was also an urban legend, which Mason never made any effort to refute, that he was even known to hold an annual event – a contest where he offered a million dollar, winner-take-all prize to swim around the Farallons during shark season – a contest where he saved filmed footage of 'eliminations' – what he supposedly called his 'highlight reel'.

Word was, his sullen mood was because there had been no sharks this year – chased out by migrating orcas. And this last season's contest was the first-ever in which there had been no highlights.

Of course, those were all just rumors.

Mason actually seemed to enjoy it.

For her part, Lindsey believed every word of it.

To see Mason sitting there in his wheelchair, a knitted quilt over his missing leg was misleading, for he remained a fearsome presence. When he rose to stand on his one good leg, he was well over six-feet and a solid, middle-aged two-hundred-and-forty pounds. Lindsey, herself, had felt the strength in his three remaining limbs – he had made sure of it.

She had actually been frightened when he'd called her this last time, to let her know he was going to be in town. Word had already filtered through of his lost shipment – something else that Lindsey wanted to know absolutely nothing about.

But oddly, by this morning, it seemed that Mason's mood had dramatically improved. She didn't know the circumstances of last night's boat accident, but Mason had been in his on-board office all day, researching online.

He had also been watching the news, playing and replaying the footage of the incident that had disrupted Beach City's annual surf rally earlier today, along with the accompanying pieces the networks were running about jumbo squid.

It seemed that Mason had discovered a new interest.

He had a taste for predators.

Lindsey found herself thinking about the rumored contest, and his first no-highlight reel year – money paid out to a winner with four unmarked survivors, and she could see it as very likely Mason might be looking for a new charge.

But it was not her place or desire to wonder about such things.

Her function was exactly what she was doing now – to lay in the sun in her bikini, and to be there when he called.

She shut her eyes, pretending to sleep, and tried not to imagine.

CHAPTER 8

Ashley spent the rest of the day online researching sea monsters.

Her producer had indeed been waiting for her call. He had already been flooded with requests for an interview with her, and he told her that getting bit by a squid was likely the biggest career boost she could have ever hoped for.

"I'm letting them bid for it," he told her.

He was also planning a special, focusing on dangerous sea creatures, which he intended to have her host.

"This is going to put you on the map," he said. "If it hits, we'll turn it into a weekly series. You'll get a different monster every week. You wanted to host your own show? This is it." He had laughed. "It's a good thing you're hot."

Ashley had absorbed this silently, exploring the possibilities in her mind.

True, becoming a sea-monster's version of Elvira wasn't exactly what she'd had in mind, but she was willing to take it.

Her producer had also suggested an interview with Brody – her hero, who their own network cameras had caught pulling her out of the squid-infested water.

"The rights to that little clip are going to go platinum," he assured her.

Ashley hadn't told Brody that part yet, but she'd taken his number after they'd shared a cab from the hospital back to the beach to retrieve both their cars.

"I'll be in touch," she told him.

"You owe me dinner," Brody reminded her.

She had also put in another call to the Oceanographic Institute up north, and had then sat down to learn everything she could about squid.

Stories about red devils, it turned out, were not hard to find. She found a website called *Release The Kraken*, hosted by a former Navy SEAL, a guy named Prescott, who had compiled attack instances from all over the world.

She watched an interview with a mother of two, who had gone diving with Humboldt squid, not far from Beach City. The woman described her initial fascination as they had circled her inquisitively, blinking their bio-luminescent lights, flashing from red to white, appearing curious, and even intelligent – an intelligence that was revealed harshly a few seconds later when she was ambushed from behind and dragged down deep.

"I remember thinking that I was going to die," the woman recounted. "I thought of my children, having their mother just... *eaten...* by *monsters*. And how horrifying that would be. And then I just began to fight for my life."

She had held up her arms, which were covered with sucker-shaped scars and small chunks taken out by the vicious beaks.

Ashley regarded her own bandaged arms, and felt a small shiver.

The SEAL who ran the site – Prescott – described a similar experience of his own, emphasizing in particular how suddenly it had become a dogfight, seventy-feet below the surface, as they had mobbed him. His arms and torso also displayed cup-shaped divots and sucker-marks.

"The first time I dived with Humboldts," he said on his video, "I got my ass kicked."

Although, as it turned out, these 'jumbo' squid were actually fairly diminutive members of the clan, which included some truly intimidating beasts.

The cover-page of *Release The Kraken* featured pen-and-ink renderings of Jules Verne's *Twenty Thousand Leagues Under The Sea* – images of the *Nautilus* submarine being attacked by a massive tentacled giant attempting to drag it down – a creature that the headline text assured the reader was very real, with documentation dating from the scientific writings of Aristotle, all the way back to the monstrous, multi-tentacled Scylla that had nearly taken down Odysseus' ship in Homer's *The Odyssey*.

While 'Kraken' was a bit of an exaggeration, as was Verne's dinosaur-sized beast – not to mention the giant animatronic monster from the Walt Disney adaptation – there was no doubt about the existence of giant squid.

"*Architeuthis dux*," Ashley recited, reading the scientific name aloud.

The more measured text, by-lined by a Professor Clyde Spencer, reported lengths of up to forty-five-feet for these beasts.

Ashley sat back in her chair, rather numb at the thought. She tried to picture the creatures that had swarmed her magnified by nearly ten times.

And fairly new on the map, and according to Professor Spencer, much more formidable, was the Colossal squid – in terms of mass, the largest invertebrate in the ocean.

She was just pulling up the page on this nasty-looking beast when her phone rang.

The ID identified the caller as Doctor Lauren Palmer – it was the Institute returning her call.

Ashley recognized Doctor Palmer's name from the news in regards to the shark attacks up in Surf Shore earlier in the season. Everett, the coroner, had sent her images of the cannibalized bodies found on the beach that morning and Doctor Palmer's verdict was unequivocal.

"Definitely not a shark attack," she said. "By my judgment, your Mr. Everett was correct. It looks like a squid."

"Do you think that's what killed them?" Ashley asked.

"No way to tell. There's so much tissue gone, it's impossible to determine the cause of death. A large squid is certainly capable of killing a human being."

That was something Ashley didn't need to be told.

"I will say," Doctor Palmer continued, "that some of these bites look a good deal larger than any Humboldt squid I've ever seen. But I'm not an expert on squid, or cephalopods in general. I'm going to refer you to a colleague."

There was a brief pause before she came on again.

"I'm sending you an email with his direct phone number," Lauren said. "Professor Clyde Spencer. He's one of the leading authorities. He works with a diver named Travis Prescott and they run a site called..."

"*Release the Kraken*," Ashley finished. "I'm looking at the page now."

"Good," Lauren said. "Last I heard, they were both working in the area. They would definitely be the ones to talk to."

"Thank you, Doctor Palmer."

"I saw that you had an incident today," Lauren said. "I'd be interested in what Professor Spencer has to say. Call me if you need anything else."

"I will," Ashley said. "Thanks again."

She was just closing her screen when her phone rang again in her hand. Brody's name popped-up.

Ashley hesitated, but tapped the screen.

"Hello?"

"Hey, girl," Brody said enthusiastically. "Ready for our second date?"

"I'm working," Ashley replied. "I'm researching squid."

"Then you'll like this," he said. "I just got a call from a fisherman friend of mine. He just pulled in a really interesting catch."

"What kind of catch?"

"Can you meet me at the docks?"

Ashley hesitated, but agreed.

"Give me half-an-hour," she said.

"See you there," Brody said, and clicked off.

Ashley stared at the phone for a moment, debating the wisdom of getting involved with this guy. Then she gathered up her keys.

She checked her watch. The docks were twenty minutes away.

Her phone beeped with the email Lauren had sent her – Professor Spencer's number.

After a moment's consideration, she brought up the number and dialed.

CHAPTER 9

When Ashley drove up, Brody was waiting for her at the pier. A mid-sized charter-fishing boat was docked and he was standing among a small circle of men, presumably the captain and the day's clients.

The 'unusual catch' turned out to be fairly prosaic – a large marlin.

What was unusual about it was that it was eaten down to the bone, just like the bodies that had washed ashore.

The group of men turned as Ashley came walking up and Brody hurried up to meet her. He looked eager and excited as if greeting her with a bouquet of roses.

Ashley suppressed a sigh. He had obviously set his camp for her. She wondered if she would end up sleeping with him after all – the five-second rule said no, but he was clearly determined, and there was always that Tequila qualifier.

In the meantime, however, she was still sober, and was content to let him run his laps as she stepped up to examine the bouquet he'd presented to her.

The captain extended his hand, introducing himself as McCormick, and he turned to the gnawed game-fish lying on the dock.

It was a good-sized marlin – over ten-feet long, and probably would have weighed eight-hundred pounds or better, except for the fact that all that remained was the head and tail, joined by a long strip of skeletonized backbone.

"We hooked it almost two-hours ago," McCormick said. "It was fighting pretty hard at first, but then the line just went heavy like an anchor. By the time we got it up, it looked like this."

"This happened while it was hooked?" Ashley asked.

McCormick ran his hands along the edges of the remaining tissue, which was lined with cup-shaped bites just like the ones on the lost boat-crew – and on Ashley's own arms. These marks, however, were much larger.

"I've seen critters eaten by squid," McCormick said. "Even giant squid. That's more than twice the size of anything I've ever seen before."

"That's because it's not a giant," a voice said from behind them. "Those bites came from a Colossal."

Two men were walking up the dock. Ashley recognized Travis Prescott and Professor Spencer from their pictures on the websites.

The two of them offered introductions all around.

Travis turned to Ashley.

"Thank you for calling us," he said. "This isn't the first evidence of large squid we've found in the area."

Professor Spencer bent over the carcass.

"Definitely a Colossal," he said. "Maybe more than one."

Captain McCormick was shaking his head.

"I've been fishing these waters for thirty years and I've never seen anything like this."

Spencer glanced grimly up at Travis as he inspected the fish carcass.

"I have," the professor said.

Travis turned to Ashley.

"I saw you on the news today, Miss Wells. I understand you had a bit of a run-in. I imagine it left a few scars."

Ashley ran her hands self-consciously over her bandaged arms.

"Those wounds," he said, "do they look anything like this?"

Travis extended his own muscular arms, which were lined with sucker-marks and beak-shaped divots.

Brody stepped forward, showing-off his own freshly-scarred arms.

"We're a matching pair," he said.

Ashley glanced sideways at Brody, who seemed to be puffing his chest.

Travis cast an amused glance at the younger man before turning back to the dead marlin.

"What do you think, Clyde?"

Spencer looked up at Captain McCormick.

"Where did you hook this guy?"

McCormick pointed south.

"Not far. About a mile past the drop-off."

Spencer turned to Travis.

"I think we should get the Coast Guard out and see what we can find. We're obviously having a boom year for Humboldts." The professor shook his head. "But this time it looks like the big ones have followed."

"Why?" Ashley asked.

Spencer shrugged.

"Food," he said. "And if the red devils are coming in close, that means the Colossals very likely could be as well."

He looked at the rest of them meaningfully.

"That could be a problem. You saw what happened today."

Ashley's hands again ran nervously down her scarred arms.

"An invasion of giant squid?"

"Not a giant squid. A Colossal," Travis corrected. "*Mesonychoteuthis hamiltoni.*"

He smiled. "I had to practice that."

"What's the difference?" Brody asked.

"Well," Travis replied. "For one thing, Colossals are bigger. A *lot* bigger actually."

Ashley blanched.

"A lot bigger than forty-five-feet?"

Travis nodded approvingly.

"You've been doing your reading. Actually, that forty-five-foot stat is misleading. More than half of that is the two longest tentacles, which is like measuring the tail of a kite."

Travis pulled out his phone and began tapping his screen.

"In terms of body mass, giant squid are a medium-to large predator. Their eight shorter arms and mantle together don't usually exceed sixteen feet, with a maximum body weight around six-hundred pounds. Roughly equivalent to a big bull shark."

Travis shook his head.

"Now that's nothing to sneeze at," he said. "And it's still quite a formidable animal. But a Colossal squid is a whole other beast."

He turned his screen so the others could see. He had brought up a picture of the two together – one a thin, elongated arrow-shape, with the other a squat, heavy, bulky mass.

"The Colossal squid is shorter, because its tentacles are shorter. But its body is much larger and more massive.

"And," he said, "it's also just a nastier piece of work."

He brought up more pictures – close-ups of the tentacles.

"Here," he said, "take a look."

The top image showed a large tentacle, labeled 'giant squid', which were lined with razor-edged suckers reminiscent of those on the smaller red devils.

Below, however, the thick, bulky arms of the Colossal were lined with taloned hooks.

"Now you tell me," Travis remarked, "which one you'd rather get grabbed by."

Ashley looked down at her bandaged arms and shivered.

"Then there's this," Travis continued, scrolling down, and then presented an image comparing beaks.

The giant squid boasted a nasty baseball-sized beak – certainly scary enough.

The beak of the Colossal posed next to it, however, was nearly the size of a soccer ball.

Ashley eyed the sharp, parrot-like jaws, glancing down again at the bandages taped over the nickel-sized nips taken from her arms.

"So what are they doing here?"

There was a flash as Professor Spencer snapped several pictures of the devoured marlin, holding his hand against the bite marks for scale.

"Well," he said, "they've not been scientifically documented in these waters before. But their range is spread across the entire southern ocean. And it's a cold jet-stream this year. They could easily be riding the colder waters north, keeping to the deep-water canyons."

The professor shrugged.

"Humboldts will often appear and disappear in places they've never been seen before. There is some evidence that the big ones run in similar cyclical patterns, although perhaps on a larger, slower scale."

"So how dangerous are they?" Ashley asked.

"Well," Travis volunteered, "imagine one of those red devils that attacked you at the beach today weighing-in at nearly a ton."

Professor Spencer nodded.

"And that's even worse if you assume a similar temperament," he said.

Now he stood away from the carcass, turning to the others.

"Even giant squid are largely unknown to science. Until recently, we didn't even know how many species there actually were. Some researchers thought there were as many as eight, some believed there was only one. A sort of consensus arose, mostly out of a spirit of compromise, suggesting three. DNA tests, however, have pretty conclusively shown that only one species exists – *Architeuthis dux* – spread throughout almost every ocean.

"We've known that for less than a decade," Spencer emphasized. "And that is with a fairly comprehensive specimen sample consisting of the remains of over a hundred-and-thirty dead individuals washed ashore, as well as tentacles and beaks retrieved from the stomachs of sperm whales.

"Colossal squid, on the other hand," the professor continued, "are edging into crypto-zoology in terms of practical knowledge, with exactly two complete specimens known."

"As to how dangerous they are? Spencer shrugged. "There *are* incidents of attacks by large squid on the books. Both on people and boats."

He pulled out his own phone, bringing up a page from *Release the Kraken*.

"There was a French ship called the *Ville de Paris* way back in 1783 that was purportedly attacked by huge squids and dragged down. In the 1930s, a Norwegian tanker reported several attacks by large squid, one that nearly managed to disable the ship's propellers."

He scrolled down, reciting the list.

"In 1941, survivors of a ship that was sunk in the South Atlantic were attacked by a large squid while clinging to a life-raft. One of the men was dragged away. Another man was attacked but fought his way loose.

"More recently," he continued, "in 2003, a yacht crew reported being attacked by a huge squid while competing in a round-the-world tour. According to the captain, the squid attached itself to the rudder, trapping the boat in place for nearly an hour before letting loose."

"What was it doing?" Brody asked. "Trying to eat the boat?"

"More likely it was a defense reaction," Travis said. "The same way they will latch onto a sperm whale."

Professor Spencer nodded. "Sperm whales eat both giant squid and Colossals."

"We've always assumed that such incidents involved giant squid specifically," Travis said. "But in terms of being able to stop or even sink a boat? *Architeuthis* simply doesn't get that big."

"There is also one case of a large squid killing a man in northern Mexico, just south of the California border, more than sixty years ago," Spencer said.

He exchanged a brief nod with Travis.

"The only witnesses were his two children. But they saw claws on the tentacles, not suckers."

Travis nodded back soberly, but said nothing.

"Legends of the Krakens have been around for centuries," Spencer said. "Many in areas where they don't appear today. Or haven't for a while.

"On the other hand, it's only been in the last hundred years or so that there would have been enough human beings out on the water to see them. And only the last couple of decades that there were enough cameras out there to take pictures."

The professor smiled ironically.

"It's kind of the opposite of Big Foot. Now that everyone's phone is a camera, no one sees Big Foot or UFOs anymore. But there's more footage of giant squid than all the rest of human history combined."

Spencer tapped off his phone.

"So," he said, "in terms of their potential danger to humans? Assuming an attitude like a Humboldt, I would say it's completely based on proximity. The legend of the Kraken taking down ships could be literally true, if the ship you're talking about is an old Viking vessel – barely twenty-five feet of hollowed-out log. One fifteen-hundred-pound beastie could slow it down or capsize it just fine. Let alone more than one.

"And remember," he said, "we're talking about numbers here. If what I suspect is true, we might be dealing with a cyclical population boom, combined with favorable conditions allowing them to come up north. And if they're following the Humboldts as a food source, then they're in feeding-mode."

Spencer glanced down at the skeletonized marlin lying on the dock.

"Imagine falling into a sea of them in the middle of a feeding frenzy," he said. "My guess is that a human being would be torn apart in seconds."

There was a brief silence as the rest of them absorbed this.

"So," Ashley said, clearing her voice uncomfortably, "what exactly should we do?"

Travis nodded out to sea.

"Well," he said, "I suggest we get on the horn to the Coast Guard and let them know what we've found. Then we get out on the water and start looking around."

Ashley glanced down at the cannibalized marlin at her feet – an eight-hundred-pound animal devoured in a sitting.

"It's for certain that they're out there," Spencer said. "The only question is how many of them there are."

Ashley looked out at the ocean and the deceptively calm waves rolling in towards shore.

Her hands again stole to the bandages on her arms. Despite the summer heat, she shivered.

CHAPTER 10

The next morning, the tide brought in what remained of Tuck and Rudy.

Ashley got the call from Lieutenant Collins to meet her down at the morgue. She in turn called Travis Prescott.

She debated whether to call Brody too. Like it or not, he was involved. Besides, the production she was putting together wouldn't be complete without a feature on the hero of the piece, who had saved the damsel from the sea monsters.

On the other hand, there was no need to encourage him.

Not today, she decided, and then her phone rang, with Brody's number popping-up.

Ashley rolled her eyes, tapping the screen.

"Did you hear?" he asked immediately.

"I heard. How did *you* know?"

"One of McCormick's friends found the bodies," Brody said. "He called me."

Ashley sighed. "Meet me at the morgue."

She dressed quickly, sending a quick text to her producer.

Ironic, she thought, just yesterday the bodies she'd seen on the beach had literally caused her to throw-up on the sand. Now she was tripping over herself to get a second look.

Her little rental house was less than a mile from the ocean and as she took the main drive that ran along the beach, Ashley found herself looking out at the water.

The Pacific was an active ocean, known for its big, cascading waves, which was what made it popular for surfing. Today, however, the breaking surf was empty.

Word had obviously gotten around. Apparently, this year, there *was* no safe zone, sharks or no sharks.

The city morgue was located in the downtown area that bordered the beach, along with the small series of municipal buildings – the courthouse and the jail. Brody was waiting for her outside, along with Travis Prescott and Lieutenant Collins. They both waved as she pulled up.

Collins smiled at her meaningfully as she got out of her car.

"I hope your stomach's feeling better today."

"It can't be any worse than yesterday," Ashley said.

Collins looked doubtful.

"Trust me. It's competitive," he said, as he led them inside.

Everett looked up as they came in.

Tank was lying on the table, recognizable from the bright red trunks that somehow still clung to his body.

The rest of him was gnawed to the bone.

Ashley paled, but this time managed to keep from gagging. It helped that she hadn't eaten today.

"Jesus," Brody whispered.

Everett nodded.

"I think we can safely rule out drowning this time," he said.

Travis leaned over the table, examining the tattered remains of soft tissue that clung to the bones.

"Humboldts," he said, indicating the smallish bites – miniature versions of the wounds on McCormick's marlin.

He nodded to Collins.

"We need to get out on the water," he said.

"I've already been on the horn to the regional office," Collins replied. "They're sending a few extra boats down to patrol. After I get out of here, I'm headed out myself." He nodded to Travis. "You're welcome to come along. I'm just a guardsman, not a scientist."

Travis nodded. "I might take you up on that."

He glanced over to the other table, still covered by a tarp.

"Both bodies pretty much in the same condition?"

"Pretty much," Everett said. "But you might want to take a look at something."

He pulled away the sheet.

Perhaps it was the sudden release of the smell but Ashley's stomach briefly rebelled.

Rudy's body was gnawed as clean as Tank's, but Everett drew their attention to several marks preserved on the bone.

These beak-marks were bigger.

"Uh oh," Brody said.

Travis bent over the corpse.

"That's no Humboldt." He looked up at the others. "This means that the Colossals were at the beach yesterday. They must have followed the Humboldts in."

Collins frowned. "That's bad, isn't it?"

Travis nodded.

"It's worse than I thought," he said. "We need to get the mayor on the phone and let him know what the situation is here."

He turned to Ashley and Brody.

"You both were luckier than you knew," he said.

Ashley looked down at the nickel-sized divots in her arms, and compared them to the melon-sized chunks taken out of the thing that used to be Rudy.

At that point, she lost the battle with her gag reflex. She turned and threw up her morning coffee into a waste basket.

Travis turned to Collins.

"Get your boys out on the water," he said. "I'm going to call Clyde and I'll meet you at the dock in one hour."

He looked down at Ashley crouched over the waste basket.

"Are you going to be alright?"

Ashley moaned. Brody nodded, kneeling beside her.

"Don't worry," Brody said. "I've had dates like this before."

"Okay," Travis said. "I'll be in touch."

He turned for the door, Collins following along behind.

Brody waited until Ashley coughed up the last of her coffee then helped her to her feet.

"I hope you're feeling better," he said, "because I've booked us a charter."

Ashley wiped her mouth. "What do you mean?"

"We're going out too. McCormick's taking us squid-fishing."

CHAPTER 11

Before heading to the dock, Travis detoured over to Mayor Vernon's office, half-a-block down the street. It was still before-hours, and the municipal buildings were not yet open, but he saw a car in the mayor's designated parking spot – a quaint, PC little eco-rig with a 'Vote Thomas Vernon' sticker on the bumper.

There was also a fancy stretch-limo parked beside him – the sort that looked like a modified mini-bus. Travis noted handicapped stickers on the license plates. As he walked past, he saw a burly fellow with bushy hair and a beard waiting in the driver's seat.

The mayor's office was a fairly modest annex to the courthouse. When Travis tried the front door, he found it unlocked.

Inside, Vernon's office light was on and the mayor was sitting at his desk.

Seated in front of him in an automated wheelchair was Colin Mason.

Travis frowned. He knew Mason by name and reputation.

Vernon looked up as Travis tapped on the door. His face appeared anxious.

"Mr. Vernon?" Travis said. "Have you got a minute?"

The mayor glanced uncomfortably at his seated guest.

"Mr. Prescott," he said, "you have news?"

"We've found the victims from yesterday, sir," Travis said, stepping up to the door.

"Yes," Vernon said, motioning him inside. "And I believe we have identified the individuals from the boat accident as well."

The mayor cleared his voice.

"Travis Prescott," he said, "meet Colin Mason."

Mason smiled mildly, reaching up to shake Travis' hand.

"My pleasure, Mr. Prescott. I've seen your documentaries. Very interesting work."

Travis shook his offered hand, noting the strength in Mason's grip.

He could see Mason sizing him up as well.

It was not the sort of look you normally got from a man sitting in a wheelchair, but Travis had seen that arch-eye before. Mason might be missing a leg, but after fourteen years in the service, Travis recognized a predator when he saw one.

There was a certain look you got once you'd deliberately killed a man hand-to-hand – let alone become proficient at it.

Mason had that look, one leg or not.

Long John Silver had one leg.

Travis guessed that Mason had twenty-pounds on him, even with the missing limb. And despite the affected aura of bloated decadence, the fat layer of wine and quality spirits was spread over a rigorously-used musculature, which in Travis' experience, was particularly dangerous in an older man, who had been using it longer.

The SEAL in him looked at Mason and saw a crafty, and very dangerous old tom-cat.

"Mr. Mason tells me it was his boat that went down the other night," Mayor Vernon said. "The two victims were his employees."

Travis nodded. A boat trip at night. The picture painted itself.

"Very unfortunate," Mason said solemnly. "They were good men. I'm here to handle their affairs on behalf of their families."

"I'm very sorry," Travis said neutrally. He turned to Vernon. "Mr. Mayor, I'm afraid we have a larger problem than we thought."

Vernon shut his eyes and Travis actually felt sorry for him. He was a little mayor of a little surf-burg, and was not psychologically equipped to handle any of this.

Still, he was the man in charge, and official channels had to go through him. Travis explained briefly.

Vernon paled as Travis showed him the images on his phone, indicating the much larger bites on Rudy's corpse.

Mason's eyes, however, seemed to glint.

"Colossal squid, you say?" Mason mused thoughtfully. "I've heard of them."

"It appears they've followed the Humboldts in this year," Travis said. "Possibly, in significant numbers."

"And what does that mean?" Vernon asked.

"It means that your surf-season is over," Travis said. "These waters aren't safe. You're going to have to close the beaches."

Vernon blanched.

"You understand that more than eighty-percent of our town's annual revenue is brought in over the course of the next few weeks. Isn't there anything we can do? Can't we go fish them out or something?"

Travis smiled a little despite himself.

"Squid populate by the thousands, Mr. Vernon. Could you catch every fish in the harbor?"

"So what do we do?" Vernon asked.

Travis shrugged.

"There's not much you *can* do, sir," he said. "These swarms come and go. All you can do is wait it out."

"For how long?"

"No telling." Travis shook his head. "Until they're gone. It could be days. It could be weeks. I'm going out with Lieutenant Collins today to scout out the waters. I might be able to get a handle on the extent of the problem after a few days. But I'm afraid there's no getting around it. Your season is over."

Vernon didn't answer, but simply nodded.

Mason sat listening, absorbing all this silently. Travis wondered briefly what his real agenda was today, coming in before-hours. He also wondered passingly if Mason might be one of Vernon's political donors. Word was, he had ownership-influence on most of the little city governments along the coast.

Travis also wondered again about the cargo of the missing boat.

Behind them, there was a knock – Mason's limo driver was standing at the door.

"Mr. Mason? I've got a call for you, sir."

Travis regarded the driver – another big man, with cold-steel eyes. Travis had heard that Mason employed a lot of mercs.

"I'll be right there, Leroy."

Mason turned to the mayor.

"Thank you for your help, Mr. Vernon," he said, tapping the lever on his wheelchair. "I'll be in touch."

He nodded to Travis. "And it was a pleasure meeting you, Mr. Prescott."

"Likewise," Travis said politely. He stepped aside, holding the door, as Mason rolled out.

Travis watched until the limo pulled away. It seemed there were more predators than just squid that had blown into town.

He turned to the mayor, sitting unhappily at his desk, and several questions dangled on the end of his tongue – queries he decided it was best not to ask.

None of my business, he thought. Stick to the predators you know.

"I'm off to the docks," he said. "I'll keep you posted."

Vernon nodded, his face etched in a morose frown.

CHAPTER 12

Ashley had never been deep-water fishing before, let alone squid-hunting.

With the images of the latest cannibalized cadavers etched firmly in her mind, her first concern was whether they had a big enough boat.

McCormick had laughed as he led her and Brody up the dock.

"I wouldn't worry, honey," he said. "We're set up to handle big game fish."

Brody nudged her.

"Try not to fall in the water, though," he said. "I don't want to have to pull you out again. Last time, I got bit."

Ashley cast him a narrowed eye as she stepped on-board.

The boat was thirty feet prow-to-stern, and solidly constructed. It smelled ripely of fish-guts.

"Have you ever done this before?" she asked.

McCormick held up a length of line, attached to what looked like some kind of medieval torture device. It was a two-foot length of metal rod, topped with what appeared to be a glow-in-the-dark bulb. Running down the length of the shaft were circles of upturned prongs, tipped in viscous-looking barbs, lined in rows.

"I picked up a few of these in Mexico a number of years back."

"What is it?"

"This is called a jig-lure. It's designed for catching Humboldts. The bulb is luminescent in the dark and attracts the squid, and when they latch on, their tentacles are caught on the barbs, and you just haul them up by hand."

He grinned.

"Fishermen in Mexico do it out of little fourteen-foot rowboats." He tapped the heavy wooden railing of his own vessel. "We ought to be just fine."

"Of course," Brody volunteered mischievously, "a few fishermen do get pulled overboard."

Ashley glared.

For a moment, she considered backing out. She hadn't even called her producer, let alone brought a camera beyond the one on her phone.

Then McCormick dropped the mooring rope attaching them to the dock and started up the motor. The boat rocked as the propellers caught, pulling away from the pier, and took them out into open water.

Ashley felt her stomach dip, reminding her she'd already thrown-up once today. She'd heard first-timers on these charters often got seasick.

As if in anticipation, McCormick reached into a cooler and handed her a can of soda.

"Where are we going?" she asked as they moved out into deeper water.

"Out past the drop-off," McCormick said. "Squid spend most of their time down deep, especially during the day, except when they come up to feed. If they're hanging around, that's probably where we'll find them."

Mercifully, the weather was good and the sea was relatively gentle. Past the breakers, the swells were large, but smooth, which was a blessing to Ashley's already-tender stomach. Once they were out on the open ocean, she began to feel better.

With the sun on her face and the wind in her hair, this was actually the sort of day she liked to be out on the water. She shut her eyes, letting herself enjoy the caress of the breeze. When she opened them again, she saw Brody smiling at her.

"What?"

"Nothing," he said. "You just really are a beautiful girl."

Ashley found herself smiling back. She'd heard variations of remarks like that her whole life and they varied from smarmy to predatory, but Brody said it with such an unaffected openness that she actually found herself charmed.

That was the thing about being genuine, she thought. It shone through.

Was she actually developing a crush?

She better stay away from that Tequila.

"Okay, Romeo," McCormick said, amused. "You want to help me get these lines out?"

McCormick dropped an anchor just at the edge of the drop-off, letting the boat drift out over the deeper water.

The ocean was crystal clear, and they could see where the underwater cliff broke away and the rocky bottom gave way to unending darkness.

Brody helped McCormick tie-off several of the wicked-looking jig-lures and tossed them over the side. The glowing lights dropped into the abyss until they were out of sight.

"It shouldn't be long," McCormick said. "If they're around, they'll bite."

Ashley looked over the railing anxiously, as if expecting a surge of red devils to come charging up at any moment.

So far, however, there was nothing.

In fact, the sea itself seemed rather subdued today, as if sleeping off the debauchery of yesterday's feeding frenzy at the beach.

McCormick shrugged.

"Give it time," he said. "Fishing's all about the waiting."

So the three of them settled down to wait.

The minutes stretched out and soon they had been waiting there for an hour and still no hits on the lines.

"Should we move further up the coast?" Brody asked.

McCormick shrugged.

"We could try, I suppose. If they're down there, they should be biting."

Ashley recalled Professor Spencer's page on *Release The Kraken*, and recalled that these swarms of Humboldts had a tendency to come and go without warning. Was it possible they had already moved on?

Her anxiousness turned to concern that her pending special might actually wind-up missing its sea monsters.

After another half-hour passed with no action, McCormick shrugged.

"Okay," he said, "pull up the lines and let's move a little further south."

Obeying himself, he grabbed the first jig-line and began to haul it up.

As he did so, there was a beeping from the cabin.

"What's that?" Ashley asked.

McCormick frowned.

"That's a GPS signal," he said.

He dropped the line back down, stepping into the cabin.

"Boats have been known to go down around here," McCormick said. "When the weather starts getting rough, the drop-off will kick the waves up, and they can flip a smaller boat pretty easily."

Ashley's ears perked. A GPS for a sunken boat?

"Why didn't we hear it before?" she asked.

"Whatever it is, it's probably gone over the edge and was being blocked by the canyon wall. We must have drifted into position to pick it up."

"Hey," Brody said, looking over the railing, "check this out."

Ashley and McCormick joined him at the port side. As the three of them peered down into the water, they could see wreckage scattered along the bottom.

Brody nodded to Ashley.

"You said a boat sank out here the other night?"

Ashley nodded.

Was this where it happened, she wondered?

"I've got it," McCormick said as the GPS continued to beep. "Looks like its somewhere right below us."

Brody smiled, looking over at McCormick, and Ashley saw the reckless look in his eye.

"You still keep diving gear on-board?" he said. "I wanna go down and take a look."

CHAPTER 13

McCormick pulled a packed bundle out on deck. Brody began unwrapping the tarp. Inside was scuba-gear and several air tanks.

"What are you doing?" Ashley asked.

Brody's grin was unabashed as he pulled one of the tanks across his back and strapped it on.

Then he picked up a second tank and handed it to Ashley.

"Come on," he said. "Let's go take a look."

Ashley shook her head. "I don't think so."

She glanced at McCormick, who seemed amused.

"Same old Brody," he said, rolling his eyes.

"Seriously," Brody said. "You're out here to investigate. Let's go investigate." His smile couldn't possibly have been broader. "Just a quick dip. In and out. Can't be more than a hundred feet to the shelf."

Ashley couldn't believe it.

"Are you kidding? It's not..." She actually found herself struggling for words. "There's *squid!*"

Brody indicated the loose lines.

"Actually, there isn't," he said. "Come on. You said you liked to dive."

"I also said I didn't dive with sharks."

"There aren't any sharks either," Brody replied cheekily. "Don't worry. I'll be there to protect you."

Ashley's eyes narrowed. Now *there* was some subtle psychology.

"What's the matter?" Brody asked, laying it on even thicker. "Scared?"

Ashley nodded back, unabashed.

"Yes," she replied.

Brody tightened the straps around his chest, cinching up the air-tank on his back.

"You've never been hurt by the ocean before," he said. "You need to get back on the horse."

He shook his head.

"This is what people do. One incident and suddenly they're scared for life. Are you just never going to go in the water again?"

"It was one incident *yesterday*."

"There were fatal car-wrecks all over the state yesterday. You drove today, didn't you?

Brody extended his arms, displaying his own sucker-marks.

"Believe it or not, I'm not a fool. I told you, I've never had a scratch before yesterday. That's called picking your moments. I've dived with Humboldts before. They're like any animal. Even piranha are only dangerous under certain conditions. We're not diving into a feeding frenzy. People swim with squid all the time."

"And there are attack-stories all over the Internet."

Brody nodded.

"Just like your Navy SEAL friend," he said. "He was attacked that first time because he went down while they were feeding. I'll bet he hasn't done *that* since."

Ashley eyed him. Is that what this was about? Was Brody trying to out-macho Travis Prescott?

"Honestly," McCormick interjected, "Brody's probably right. Humboldts follow the bait-fish. That's how they ended up at the beach yesterday. And they weren't attacking people so much as the people got caught in the way."

He nodded over the side where the underwater cliff dropped off into the depths.

"They tend to hang down deep during the daytime. To the tune of twenty-thousand-feet or better. And we haven't had a bite all day."

But he smiled ruefully.

"Don't get me wrong," he said, "*I* wouldn't do it."

"Tell you what," Brody said, pulling on his mask. "You pull this, and dinner's back on me."

Then he pulled out a little GoPro camera and attached it to the mask, clicking it on and zooming in on her.

"And you're going to be on-camera," he said, smiling.

Ashley eyed him back. His methods were not exactly subtle.

She looked down at the water, clear and so comfortingly empty. She took a breath.

"Okay," she said.

CHAPTER 14

As McCormick helped Ashley strap on her air-tank, he smiled reassuringly.

"Seriously, Miss," he said, "I wouldn't let this happen if I thought it was unsafe." He nodded at Brody. "I've known this kid a long time and he really isn't crazy."

And then, confidentially, "But I think he wants you to think he is."

Ashley smiled back nervously.

McCormick tightened her last strap with a pat.

"But don't do it if you don't feel comfortable."

Ashley glanced over at Brody, who was waiting expectantly.

Was she really going to do this? McCormick was giving her a chance to back out.

But she nodded.

"I'm okay," she said.

Brody smiled as he let himself fall over the side, hitting the water with a splash.

Ashley put in her mouthpiece and took a deep breath of compressed air. Then she jumped in after him.

The moment she hit the water, she felt Brody there beside her, reaching out to take her hand. He drew her gently down next to him.

Brody held them there a moment, giving her a moment to breathe, letting the weightless drift of being underwater calm her, his fingers entwined with hers as if inviting her to dance.

He took a moment to adjust his GoPro, focusing in on her like a fashion photographer.

Ashley found herself smiling despite herself. He really was smooth.

As they paused, drifting under the surface, she realized she actually felt very safe in his company.

She couldn't deny it anymore – his roguish charm was working on her. She was starting to fall for him. And with nary a bottle of Tequila in sight.

Now Brody pointed down, and then touched two fingers together in an *okay* sign.

Ashley's heart tapped a bit faster, but she nodded.

The two of them followed the anchor-line down. The water was perhaps a hundred feet deep before the drop-off and Brody took them down slowly. The ocean floor below was rocky, sans vegetation, like a desert canyon that had sunk beneath the sea.

They could see scattered wreckage lying across the bottom, but there was no boat. The angle of the debris rather resembled the path of a car-wreck, leaving pieces of itself behind, before going over the cliff. The current must have carried it over the edge.

As they touched bottom, Brody began picking at the bits of scrap – a section of railing, what looked like part of the stern. There was also a larger chunk of equipment that Ashley realized was the boat's motor, separated and loose.

Brody drifted over the top, examining the broken piece of machinery, focusing in with his GoPro.

Dug into the sides of the motor were deep, jagged scratch marks. Brody ran his hands over them – they were wider than his fingers.

They looked like the claw marks of a tiger.

Ashley felt a touch of doubt as she looked around the surrounding water.

Brody motioned for her to pose in front of the disembodied motor. She held her fingers beside the claw-marks for scale.

They followed the trail of wreckage towards the drop-off. Ashley could see the open darkness beyond. She hoped Brody wasn't planning on exploring over the edge.

But as they drew closer, she spotted something odd.

Scattered among the debris were what at first looked like small pillows wrapped in plastic. But as they drew closer, she could see they were actually sealed packets of white powder.

Brody picked one of them up, tearing the plastic and letting the contents swirl into the current.

Now he turned to her, and she could see his eyes had gone wide behind his face-mask.

Ashley realized what she was looking at, and remembered whose boat this must have been. She had never heard of Colin Mason before, but Lieutenant Collins had told her he was someone she didn't want to know.

Brody shook the bag empty, letting the water wash the white powder away.

Cocaine? Heroin, perhaps?

Either way, Brody's demeanor had suddenly changed. As he let the bag float, he took her hand more firmly, pointing to the dissipating powder. He shook his head assertively, and drew his finger in a slashing motion across his throat.

No adrenaline-junkie now, he pointed urgently back towards the surface.

Ashley understood well enough. This wasn't something they wanted to find. Brody pulled at her hand, turning back towards the anchor-line.

But as they started to make their way across the bottom, they looked up to see the churning wake of a second boat arriving on the scene – a much larger vessel, pulling up beside McCormick's charter boat.

Ashley and Brody exchanged glances. Behind his mask, Brody's eyes were wide.

Seeing the look in his eyes, Ashley felt a tremor of fear.

When she had entered the water, her primary concern had been the wildlife. But as she glanced back to the dozens of scattered packets lying about the sea floor, this was something she hadn't considered.

Brody paused, looking up doubtfully at the surface above.

As if sensing the mood, the light itself seemed to fade.

Ashley blinked – for a moment, it looked as if a cloud had settled over the sun – except this was a cloud moving below the surface.

There was a shimmer of reflective light.

A school of bait-fish, Ashley realized, was moving in from the ocean, from out over the drop-off.

Just like yesterday at the beach.

Her grip on Brody's hand grew tight.

CHAPTER 15

Up on the surface, McCormick kept a careful eye on the jig-lines.

He was a little nervous. Truthfully, he didn't believe there was any excessive danger beyond that normally associated with diving in the open ocean. Anytime you dropped a hundred feet below the water with nothing but a two-foot tank of air to keep you alive, going down deep enough where you couldn't even quickly swim back to the surface for air without blowing out your lungs, you were taking an inherent risk.

But today was a paid charter, and that made him liable. He'd known Brody since he was a teenager and the kid was as adept in the water as a seal, and McCormick knew the young lady was as safe in his company as a licensed instructor or a lifeguard.

Still, there *had* been an unusual incident yesterday – not an unprecedented one, for Humboldt squid had passed through the area in years past. But there had never been fatalities involved before. And while McCormick chalked that mostly up to happenstance and bad luck, in his experience, those things had a tendency to run together.

There was also that devoured marlin. Granted, they had pulled that line up from down deep, but it was evidence that conditions in the area were oddball this year.

He knew he was probably being overly skittish – the fact was that there weren't even any sharks this season, which meant it was probably even safer than normal.

Nonetheless, he would feel better once Brody took his date home tonight.

McCormick smiled a little at the thought – the young lady didn't even seem quite aware that it *was* a date. But to his eyes, it looked like Brody was winning her over. The kid knew how to make an impression, and a hundred-foot wreck-dive beat the hell out of dinner and a movie.

Ah, to be young again.

Idly, he checked the GPS signal. He wondered if they would find anything down there. The currents at the drop-off tended to wash any clutter over the edge into the deeper canyons. But whatever they found, McCormick was sure Brody would treat it like buried treasure.

So far, that was the extent of the excitement for the day, because the ocean seemed utterly empty.

That was just how it was sometimes. He'd done enough fishing to know there were days when the ocean-life just wasn't in evidence. Somewhere, he was sure, there were schools of fish crowding and feeding, probably in the thousands, and probably not far off, but for whatever reason, they had taken a different direction today. There had not been many fishing days where he'd been completely skunked, but it *had* happened.

He settled down to wait, lulled by the roll of the waves, but keeping a careful eye on the jig-lines.

And then, almost masked by the soft rustle of the wind, McCormick's sensitive ears picked-up another sound – the drone of an approaching motor.

He stood up, covering his eyes against the sun, looking out over the water.

Off in the near-distance, moving in their direction, was a boat.

Pulling out a pair of binoculars, he focused in.

He had been expecting to see a Coast Guard patrol – Brody had mentioned they were out touring the coastline today, in the aftermath of yesterday's incident – but this was a much bigger boat. It looked like a pretty fancy yacht.

McCormick frowned. He had seen this particular yacht before, and he knew who it belonged to.

Colin Mason was well-known among the fishing community, and he was given a wide berth.

Belatedly, a number of connections rattled off in his head. For the first time, it occurred to him to wonder whose boat might have gone down out here the other night.

A cold finger touched down on his chest.

What if there was something down there that Brody and his girl weren't supposed to find?

There was no doubt the yacht was moving in their direction, and McCormick realized it was probably honing in on the same GPS signal he had picked-up on.

And they were out here all alone.

Setting down the binoculars, McCormick pulled out his phone and pulled up the number for the Coast Guard.

From the cabin behind him, his radio beeped. A hailing frequency from the approaching boat.

"Oh boy," he whispered. He looked down at the water after Brody.

As he did so, he had the impression of a cloud passing just below the surface.

There was a sparkle of silvery bodies, and McCormick realized it was a large school of bait-fish, moving in towards shore from the deep water.

Just like yesterday.

A moment later, one of the jig-lures jerked abruptly.

Then another.

McCormick glanced up at the approaching yacht, and then back down in the water. From the cabin, the radio continued to beep.

He tapped the Coast Guard emergency number and began typing out a message, even as he reached for the radio.

Bad luck and happenstance, he thought. All running together.

They might be in trouble.

CHAPTER 16

As Ashley and Brody looked up from the ocean floor, the cloud of bait-fish blocked out the sun. And on the surface, moving in next to the little fishing schooner, the second boat pulled up alongside – a much larger vessel – clearly not a Coast Guard boat.

Ashley looked around the rocky bottom at the little packs of packed powder.

No one you want to know, Lieutenant Collins had said.

There was no way to quantify how foolish she felt right at that moment. She was tempted to be angry at Brody, but instead, she instinctively drew closer to him. He gave her hand a squeeze.

For the moment, they held their place, looking up at the surface.

Among the schooling bait-fish, they began to see flashes of blinking red lights.

The red devils were following their food.

Ashley watched helplessly. They hadn't dived into a feeding frenzy. One had swum right up on top of them.

Brody floated, indecisively, checking the meter on his air-tank, and then tapped Ashley's arm, motioning for her to check her own.

Her heart was hammering. She was using her air up too fast.

Brody turned her towards him, holding up his hand in a calming gesture.

Ashley took a deliberately slow breath, trying to let her body relax. Brody held her hand, keeping her eyes focused on him. Finally, her heart-rate began to slow.

Brody nodded reassuringly. Then he pointed to the anchor-line. Ashley shut her eyes, steeling herself, then nodded back.

Together, they began crawling along the bottom, making their way over to the anchor. Brody grabbed the tether, looking up at the surface, which was now clouded with both fish and Humboldts, and he motioned to go slow. Ashley nodded affirmatively.

Hand-over-hand, they began to pull themselves up along the anchor-line, back towards the surface, consciously moving slower than their slowest bubble. The light seemed to grow dimmer as they moved closer to the living, moving cloud above.

And then suddenly the fish were schooling around them, the wake of their passage rustling like a passing breeze. And among the fish were the Humboldts, pulsing steadily with bio-luminescence.

Ashley felt her heartbeat ticking back up again. As if sensing it, Brody gave her fingers a brief squeeze, holding up his hand. Ashley shut her eyes, forcing herself calm.

The squid were still cruising among the crowding drove of bait-fish, as if corralling them – they hadn't actually started feeding yet, perhaps waiting for some group signal to start moving in.

Ashley hoped that was a good thing. Travis Prescott had a lot of footage on his website, swimming with them unmolested, having learned his lesson after being attacked that first time. As he put it, his fundamental principle with all predatory animals was 'don't act like prey'.

That, and don't jump into the middle of their dinner table.

There was a flash of red and a blur of movement as the first of the squid suddenly darted forward, its tentacles snaking out, snagging one of the schooling fish. In a moment, the others followed suit. Almost as one, the Humboldts moved in and began to feed.

Brody held up his hand, motioning to stay still as the stout, five-foot bodies went scooting by, ignoring them, at least for the moment. Ashley felt the bump of small bodies as the bait-fish fled past.

They hung there motionless. Ashley looked to the surface, still so very far away. Brody waited as the passing parade split to either side, as both predator and prey went flying past.

Finally, he nodded, and they began to move again, pulling themselves along the rope. They ascended excruciatingly slowly, but now they were finally drawing near the surface.

Then, in the corner of her eye, Ashley saw the shadow of something larger.

At first, it was just a dark mass, but then there was a flickering pulse of light. Ashley's heartbeat kicked up again, and she pulled on Brody's arm, pointing down.

The larger shape had already moved out of sight. Brody shook his head. He had missed it. But Ashley could see his eyes through the mask as he looked back at her grimly, pointing urgently toward the surface.

Ashley nodded and they had just started to move again, when one of the circling Humboldts suddenly darted in and grabbed her by the arm.

The saw-blade suckers dug into her skin, and Ashley screamed into her mouthpiece as she felt the digging beak.

But Brody moved just as fast. He jumped in, punching at the eyes, pulling the grasping tentacles away from her arm. The squid released her, turning its attention to Brody as he wrestled the thing away.

The moment he pushed off from the anchor-line, three more rushed him. Brody battled back, kicking and punching, as they mobbed him. Two of them let go and skirted away, but the third continued to hang-on tenaciously.

Ashley had started to move in to help when suddenly a massive dark shape lit up from below like electric neon.

The huge mass was nearly five feet across as it darted upwards, and seemed to split apart as two elongated tentacles lashed out like a lizard's tongue, followed by grasping, taloned arms that spread out more than fifteen feet across. In the middle of the squirming mass, Ashley saw a giant cleaving beak larger than her head.

There was a twin flash of ambulance-red as the tentacles snagged the red devil clinging to Brody's arm, drawing the smaller squid into the chomping jaws.

Brody pushed away, turning back to Ashley, his eyes wide behind his mask, his arms slashed and bleeding. Around them, there was a brief pause as the Humboldts pulled back in a flock. Brody pointed desperately to the surface as he started to kick back towards the anchor-line.

Then there was another flash of red as a second massive shape suddenly lunged.

This time, the two reaching tentacles grabbed Brody across the torso.

In an instant, he was drawn back into the grasping tentacles and pulled into the chomping beak. There was an explosion of bubbles as his air-tank was ruptured. Ashley could see him fighting wildly.

Then clouds of blood began to mix with the bubbles.

Brody's struggles abruptly ceased. His body went limp and Ashley watched him drawn down into the dark.

Panic shot a highball of adrenaline into her veins. Abandoning all caution, Ashley began kicking desperately for the surface.

Now she was acting like prey. And the Humboldts treated her accordingly.

The red devils swarmed. She felt two of them latch onto her air-tank even as several more came darting up, grasping at her legs. Both of her swim-fins were pulled loose as she kicked away.

She pulled at the straps across her chest, releasing the tank from her back. The two squid fell away, both clinging to the loose cylinder, fighting for their prize. A second later, there was an explosion of air as the tank burst.

There was another brief pause as one of the red devils fluttered drunkenly, stunned by the blast. The other floated limply.

Then one of the larger shapes moved up from below. Ashley saw the two long tentacles launch out.

She actually felt them strike her, knocking her aside as they snatched the struggling Humboldt – the one that was still alive – drawing it down into the grasping arms and beak.

The next moment, a swarm of red devils darted in, grabbing hold of the second, and began tearing it apart.

In the moment's reprieve, Ashley again began kicking towards the surface. Beneath her was a kaleidoscope of flashing red lights.

Even as her head broke the surface, she again felt herself grabbed from below as the Humboldts latched onto her bare legs. She kicked, choking water, spitting out her mouthpiece, and she began to scream.

"Help me!"

Her mask had been knocked ajar and was full of water, leaving her blinded. She thrashed wildly, and then suddenly her head impacted solidly against something hard.

It was the hull of one of the boats. The blow knocked her dizzy and she went limp in the water.

Then she felt herself grabbed again.

But this time it was from above, a heavy hand gripping her arm. In a single movement, she was yanked bodily from the water.

Still blinded, she felt herself thrown down onto hard wood. As she coughed up water, she gasped until she caught air, pulling away her mask, her eyes tearing.

When her vision cleared, she saw a bearded man looking down at her, big and broad-shouldered. His eyes were cold and hard.

The man looked over his shoulder.

"Got her, Mr. Mason," he said.

As she sat up, Ashley looked around to find herself sitting on the deck of a large yacht.

Seated in a wheelchair, watching with interest, was a man with one leg.

"Welcome aboard, Miss," Colin Mason said.

CHAPTER 17

Ashley wondered if she'd been saved after all.

Blood ran down her arms and legs onto the hardwood deck, but none of the men standing about made any move to offer aid. The big fellow with the bushy beard who had fished her out simply stood, looking down at her impassively – and not with the eyes of a rescuer so much as a man who had just landed a trout. Or perhaps a bear who had just yanked a salmon out of the river – one that he intended to eat.

But that was better than the look in Colin Mason's eyes. His expression was a comfortable, easy smile, but those *eyes*...

A young woman in a bikini stood behind Mason's chair, perched over his shoulder – a position of obvious purpose as she massaged and caressed his neck like an attentive Geisha. She was Ashley's age or younger and her own eyes were deliberately distant.

Three more large hominids filled out the rest of the crew, varying in detail but otherwise indistinguishable from the bear-like creature who had hauled her from the water.

The yacht had pulled up intimidatingly close beside the little fishing boat, and McCormick was leaning over the rail.

"Ashley?" he called over. "Are you alright? Where's Brody?"

Her voice hitched once in an abbreviated sob.

"They... got him," she stammered. "A *big* one. He's gone."

The bear-man looked over the railing.

"Hey, boss," he said, "I think you're going to want to get a look at this."

The young woman pushed Mason's chair over to the railing. Gingerly, affecting the appearance of infirmity, Mason hopped up on his one leg – but Ashley noted the spring in the movement and the flex of muscle as he stood and looked out into the water.

Cruising beneath the waves, visible among the darting bait-fish and the swarming red devils, were much larger shapes, flashing red like emergency lights.

"Interesting," Mason said. "Very interesting."

He glanced down at Ashley, sitting curled and bleeding on the deck.

"That's what took your friend?"

Ashley nodded mutely.

Mason shook his head in theatrical regret.

"I think you're very lucky to be alive, Miss... Wells, isn't it? I recognize you from the news reports yesterday."

And now Mason turned, regarding her directly.

"I don't suppose you happened to see anything else down there, did you? Like perhaps a sunken boat?"

Ashley looked up at him wide-eyed, afraid to speak.

"I'll take the lady aboard," McCormick called over, speaking up quickly. "She needs medical attention."

Mason held up his hand. "One moment please."

McCormick frowned.

Mason looked down at Ashley expectantly.

"Well," she said, swallowing nervously. "We picked-up a GPS signal. And Brody... he wanted to go check it out."

"And what did you find?"

Ashley shook her head.

"We saw pieces of wreckage," she said. "We found a boat motor."

She paused a moment, remembering.

"It was marked up. Like with *claws*."

She looked down at her fingers which had so easily fit in the carved-out grooves.

Mason nodded.

'Mesonychoteuthis hamiltoni," he said as he looked back out over the water. The words rolled smoothly off Mason's cultured tongue – not the deliberate pronunciation of Travis Prescott, but the accent of a man who spoke many languages, probably from business dealings all over the world – businesses like those that supplied those scattered packets of white powder.

"Colossal squid," Mason mused. "I've developed a bit of an overnight interest in the species. Claw-marks on the motor, you say? That's *very* interesting."

He let go of the railing and settled back into his chair. The woman in the bikini immediately resumed her steady massage.

Ashley caught the woman's eye. Her pretty, painted face was carefully neutral, but now it seemed that a shadow passed behind her eyes – a flinch. Ashley was uncertain if it was masking concern, or possibly apprehension at what she might be about to witness.

"Did you see anything else down there?" Mason asked mildly.

Ashley shook her head.

"I think the main wreck went over the drop-off."

"That is unfortunate," Mason said, shaking his head. "I had valuable cargo aboard. And that water is quite deep. I imagine anything that went over that edge would be as good as lost forever."

His eyes narrowed.

"*Anything*," he said.

The woman behind him shut her eyes briefly at the tone. Her expression turned to one of sympathy – fading a moment later as if remembering herself.

Ashley curled herself into a ball, pulling her bleeding limbs close.

She glanced over at McCormick, who was watching the scene apprehensively. His hands had disappeared beneath the railing, as if reaching for something unseen.

Then there was the sound of a boat horn.

Approaching from the north was a Coast Guard security boat.

With an audible sigh of relief, McCormick let go of whatever he had been holding out of sight, and his hand came back into view.

Sitting back into his chair, Mason also seemed to relax – a panther settling back from a prepared leap. His comfortable Cheshire cat smile returned.

Lieutenant Collins was leaning on the front railing as the Guard boat slowed. Standing beside him was Travis Prescott.

"Afternoon everybody," Collins called out as they pulled up next to the two anchored boats. "Are we crashing a party?"

"Lieutenant Collins," Mason called back. "How very nice to see you."

"I wish I could say the same, Mr. Mason," Collins replied. "What are you doing out here?"

"Well," Mason replied, "it seems that Captain McCormick here has located our lost boat."

"And I suppose you're here for a responsible salvage operation?" Collins volunteered. "On behalf of your shipping company?"

Mason's smile widened.

"Of course."

"Right." Collins glanced sideways at Travis, who responded with a none-of-my-business shrug.

"Unfortunately," Mason said, "it looks like we are facing a bit of an obstacle." He indicated the water. "Have a look."

Collins and Travis both looked over the railing. Down in the water, the traveling light-show continued to sail past, ignoring the boats above.

They could clearly see the larger shapes moving among them.

"Jesus," Collins whistled.

"Colossals," Travis said. He shook his head. "I've never seen anything like this."

"I'm afraid," Mason continued, "that your friends have suffered a bit of a loss."

Ashley caught Travis' eye as she still sat sprawled on Mason's deck, dripping blood.

"Ashley," Travis said. "What happened?"

She nodded over the railing.

"They took Brody," she said, and now tears began to stream down her face. "He's dead."

Travis' face darkened. He nodded to Lieutenant Collins, who looked over his shoulder to the pilot, who tapped the motor, drifting them in close to Mason's yacht.

Travis extended his hand to Ashley.

"Come on," he said. "Let's get you home."

"We would be happy to take her in," Mason volunteered.

"I'm sure you would," Collins replied. "But I'm also sure she's not that kind of girl."

The woman standing over Mason's shoulder frowned.

Ashley took Travis' hand and let herself over the railing onto the Guard boat.

Travis turned his eye to Mason's crew of mercs. The troop of them stared back, their robotic-cyborg eyes unblinking.

"Thank you for your help, Mr. Mason," Travis said politely.

Mason smiled back winningly. "Of course."

"And," Collins added, "I think the authorities can handle the salvage from here. Any valuables recovered will, of course, be returned to you."

Mason's Cheshire cat smile grew thin.

"Of course."

Ashley huddled on the floor of the Guard boat. Travis knelt beside her, examining the fresh wounds on her arms and legs.

"Are you alright, honey?"

Ashley shut her eyes, squeezing out tears.

"They took him," she said again. "They *ate* him."

Travis nodded.

"Let's get you to a doctor," he said.

Collins waved to McCormick.

"Captain McCormick, if you wouldn't mind following us in, we're going to need a statement from you concerning what happened to Brody."

McCormick made an okay sign, glancing back at Mason, as he started up his motor.

Mason made a hand-gesture and, as if by telekinesis, the yacht's motor started up as well.

"We'll be in touch, Mr. Mason," Collins called out, eyeing him meaningfully. "And we will let you know what we find."

"Thank you, Lieutenant," Mason replied.

The yacht began to pull away, leaving the other two boats behind.

Travis' eyes narrowed, as he watched the big boat turn north, maintaining a steady distance from shore. Mason clearly wasn't headed to port.

"What do you think he's got in mind?" Travis asked Collins.

The lieutenant shook his head.

"I think these waters just got a lot more dangerous," Collins replied. "And it has nothing to do with giant squid. I'll take a Kraken over that sonofabitch any day."

Travis nodded grimly, his face etched in a frown.

CHAPTER 18

"This is twice in a week," Travis said, "When are you going to learn?"

Ashley nodded silently as the nurse worked on her wounds – the same woman who had treated her yesterday. She was even given the same hospital bed.

"For what it's worth," Travis said, "I'm sorry about Brody. I could tell that you liked him."

"I barely knew him," Ashley said.

But even as she said it, she knew it didn't matter. The truth of it was that he had charmed her. In the two days since he had first saved her life, she'd managed to develop an unwilling crush. He had even saved her life for a second time right there at the end. Granted, he'd talked her down there in the first place, but she'd gone willingly enough.

It seemed so foolish now. In retrospect, the *why* of it escaped her. A career move? Just so she could add drama to her documentary?

Or had it been her own response to simple flirting?

Silly and ridiculous, either way. And now Brody was gone.

Travis didn't push the point, but he could see well enough.

The nurse sat back, replacing the last bandages.

"You should be fine," she said. "These wounds aren't deep. But you're probably going to see some scarring."

Inside and out, Ashley thought, but she nodded.

The nurse's eyes were sympathetic.

"Try to take it easy for a few days," she said. "I'd hate to see you back in here again. But beyond that, I'd say you're fine to go home."

The nurse nodded politely to Travis, who waited for her to leave before sitting down next to Ashley's bed, looking at her confidentially.

"About that," he said. "I'm not sure if going home is such a good idea."

"What do you mean?"

"What I mean is that it might be advisable for you to get out of town for a few days."

His eyes were very serious.

"You saw something down there besides squid, didn't you?"

Ashley said nothing, but she nodded.

"I've been talking to Lieutenant Collins," Travis said, "and he tells me Colin Mason does a pretty brisk shipping business off the coast of southern California. I'm guessing the boat that went down was carrying highly illegal cargo."

"We saw packets of white powder," Ashley said. "Scattered all over the bottom."

Travis sighed. "Pretty much what I thought."

He glanced over his shoulder, making sure no one was within earshot.

"According to Lieutenant Collins, Mason doesn't like loose-ends. What if he decides it's uncomfortable for you to be alive?"

Ashley said nothing. But she remembered the look on Mason's face as he had grilled her about what she'd seen – as she sat huddled and bloody on the deck of his yacht.

Travis shook his head.

"Collins has a good idea what was on that boat," he said. "And he said he was going to talk to Chief Mathews, as well as the State Police and the Feds. But don't think for a moment that makes you safe. In fact, if Mason gets wind of it, that could very easily make things worse."

Ashley stared back wide-eyed.

"At the moment," Travis continued, "conditions around the site are considered too dangerous to attempt a recovery operation. And it could very well be, by the time anyone official gets around to getting down there, the currents could take any evidence over the drop-off."

He shrugged.

"That might make Mason feel safe," he ventured. "*Or*, it could mean he might look at you as the only living witness."

Ashley swallowed dryly. She couldn't believe what she was hearing.

Get out of town? And go where? For how long? She had exactly three months' worth of income saved and that was based on paying rent, not motel bills.

And really, with Mason's obvious resources and reach, where would a safe-haven be?

"There's also the possibility," Travis continued, "that Mason might attempt a recovery himself. Collins thinks that's what he had in mind today. The incident with Brody might have derailed that. But..."

Travis leaned in close.

"Collins says that Mason is crazy. Some of the things he told me, just the things they suspect, are... pretty bad. He says he honestly can't predict what Mason will do."

Ashley nodded. That decided her.

"Okay," she said. "I'll get out of town."

She almost couldn't believe she was saying the words – that she actually found herself in this situation.

"Smart girl," Travis said. "I would get in your car, and just get yourself lost. Find a motel for tonight. And then find another one tomorrow. Keep moving."

"I'll be broke in two-weeks," Ashley said.

Travis shrugged. "Beats the alternative."

"What am I supposed to do? Just stay on the run forever?"

"I'll keep in touch. Collins will keep in touch, and we'll see what Chief Mathews says. And you might be talking to the State cops or the Feds soon."

Protective custody, Ashley thought numbly.

Suddenly, her whole life had changed. It had just been since yesterday.

As she sat there in her little hospital bed, she suddenly felt very alone. Very small. A trickle of a tear rolled down one cheek.

Travis reached out and touched her hand.

"Come on. Let's get you out of here. I'll take you home."

CHAPTER 19

Lindsey was afraid. Never in her life had she been more afraid.

She had just spent her first evening alone with Mason in his personal suite on-board the yacht. She had known before now that his tastes in the bedroom ran heavily towards fear and dominance, but what had gone on in his room last night had been *unspeakable*.

The rumors that Lindsey had heard about Colin Mason, even after knowing him for four years, were far different than being confronted with confirmed reality.

For example, his 'Contest' – his annual race through the Farallon Islands during shark season. Last night, she had seen his 'highlight reels'.

As Mason put it, it was the only race in the world where the highlights were comprised of the eliminations.

It wasn't all that different than the *Air Jaws* videos Lindsey herself had watched on the Discovery channel, with massive Great Whites breaching, hitting targets on the surface at upwards of thirty-miles an hour, rocketing their two-ton bodies more than fifteen feet clear of the water.

Only these sharks weren't attacking seals. And they weren't decoys.

Mason had made Lindsey watch the videos with him.

And then he had *done* things to her.

Before last night, she had just worked for him. But she was his property now.

Because after what she had seen last night, she knew she would never be allowed to leave his service. If she ever tried, that would make her a loose-end – she would become someone he couldn't trust.

With the absence of sharks in the Farallons to provide this year's highlights, Mason had actually been delighted with the appearance of the Humboldts, let alone the giant Colossals. The lost cargo was a secondary concern.

That reporter lady who Mason's goon had pulled out of the water today had no idea how lucky she was to be alive.

For Lindsey, the only psychological defense was to hide away inside herself and lock it away forever.

Now, as the sun set, she lay on her lawn chair, stretched out in her bikini. As was her job.

Mason sat at the stern railing. The yacht was at anchor, only a few miles north from where the boat had gone down.

Two of Mason's mercs were feeding fish-guts into the water, in the manner of attracting sharks. This year, the first thing that appeared were schools of bait-fish.

It wasn't long before the red devils followed.

Lindsey knew they were called red devils. She had learned a lot about squid in the last day or so, as Mason prattled-on, almost like a kid, eager to share all the recently-acquired knowledge of his new and sudden interest.

In its way, it *was* fascinating.

There was something remarkable about bio-luminescence. The darting Humboldts were like the glow-in-the-dark toys she'd had as a kid. Watching them zoom about under the surface was a little bit magical – albeit a dark, sorcerous magic.

Mason's men had put out a couple of jig-lures and both of them began to jerk on their mooring. Leroy, the big bear-looking fellow, who seemed to be Mason's head goon, grabbed one of the lines and began hauling it up. A second merc, with a bushy red-beard, who Mason had yet to call by name, started pulling in the second line.

Before long, Lindsey saw the first of the struggling squid, flashing red as it was drawn near the surface. When it was within ten feet, Mason held up his hand.

"Hold it. Leave it there."

After a moment, the squid's fellows came mobbing in, attacking and cannibalizing the struggling creature, and within moments had torn it apart.

A second Humboldt was dragged up a minute later and suffered the same fate.

They eat their own, Lindsey thought, and shuddered.

Mason watched, his eyes slit like a cat's.

It was rather like the look he'd worn last night, while watching his highlight reels – just before he'd turned his attention to *her*.

Now he smiled, waving her over.

"Come here," he said. "Take a look at this."

Lindsey took an involuntary breath. For some reason, he liked her to watch.

Obediently, she joined him at the railing.

Hopping out of his chair on one foot, Mason stood up next to her, his hand steeling to the back of her neck, caressing gently.

Then abruptly, he grabbed her by the arm and threw her over the side.

Lindsey hit the water before she even drew a breath to scream.

Out this far, the ocean was blood-chilling cold.

Lindsey felt the bumping passage of the schooling fish, and in the dark, she could see the flashing red pulses of the Humboldts. She thrashed in the water, struggling for the surface.

When her head broke water, she found her scream.

There was no use crying for help. Instead, she cried out, "*Please!*"

The underwater boat lights came on, illuminating the water, and Lindsey knew there were cameras filming.

She could see Mason's face as he watched, and the look in his eyes was hungrier than it had ever been during sex.

Lindsey felt a sudden impact, followed by pain in her arm as sucker-laden tentacles latched onto her arm, and then a sharper pain as the beaks sank into her soft skin.

Now she just screamed unintelligibly, an outburst of outrage and horror, and she began to fight.

She felt herself grabbed by the other arm, and then by both legs.

The illuminated water began to cloud red with her blood. She tried to scream again, but choked water as she was pulled beneath the surface.

Lindsey could see the lights of the boat fading as she was pulled down into the deep.

She had already fought herself to exhaustion, and her lungs were ready to burst. Her struggles weakened until the moment she finally inhaled water.

There were a few last moments of consciousness, where she felt the squid beginning to feed on her flesh, before the world went mercifully black.

Staring down from the railing, Mason nodded approvingly to Leroy and red-beard.

"That was pretty good," he said.

Mason shut his eyes for a moment, and let out a deep, satisfied sigh.

When he opened them, it was back to business.

"The reporter lady," he said. "Get her. Bring her to me."

CHAPTER 20

When Travis took Ashley home, Chief Mathews was waiting for them in her driveway.

"I called ahead," Travis told her. "He's going to keep an eye on you until you get your bags packed."

Ashley looked at the two of them soberly.

"You think Mason is going to come after me tonight?"

"I don't know," Travis said."It's better to play it safe."

Mathews looked concerned.

"Mason's crazy," he said.

Ashley shut her eyes, taking a breath.

"Okay. Give me a few minutes."

Travis took her hand.

"You've got my number," he said. "Let me know where you end up." He pulled out his wallet and handed her his credit card. "Here. Use this to sign in. That way he can't track you."

Ashley smiled back shakily.

"What's my limit?"

Travis smiled. "Enough for a motel for a few nights." He tapped the card. "I *do* want it back."

Ashley nodded gratefully. Travis turned to Mathews.

"Keep an eye on her."

Mathews nodded.

Travis gave Ashley's hand one last squeeze, then turned back to his car. He leaned out the window as he pulled away.

"Keep me posted," he said.

Ashley waved, before turning to Mathews. The police chief smiled reassuringly.

"I'll wait out here while you pack," he said.

Ashley let herself into her little rented house – her first actual house, not an apartment. She'd been so proud to be able to afford it once she'd gotten the local network job.

As she began to pack her bag, she started crying.

The tears came fast and hard, and Ashley could actually feel her mind separate, like an out-of-body experience, where she seemed to look back at herself like a bystander, wondering whether it was grief over Brody, the trauma of her own injuries, or simply all of it together, piled on top of now possibly becoming the target of a wealthy psycho.

She was glad Travis was gone and that Mathews waited outside. She wouldn't have wanted *anyone* to see her like this. She felt so weak and helpless – and bizarrely, the feeling was a lot like shame, as if she deserved this for acting like a fool.

It was several minutes before she was able to bring herself under control.

Finally, the storm ended. Rising resolutely to her feet, she turned to the bathroom to wash her face.

A few days in a motel, she thought. But what then? It wasn't as if Mason was not going to still be out there. And men like him had a long reach.

That was the thought on her mind when she heard the creak on the floorboard in the hallway outside her bedroom.

She knew that board. It absolutely never creaked unless someone stepped on it.

Ashley's heart stopped.

Had someone already been waiting in her house? With Chief Mathews still waiting outside?

She had no gun in the house – she didn't believe in them until about ten seconds ago.

Ashley watched paralyzed as the door to her bedroom slowly opened. She saw the shadow outside and sucked in her breath for a scream.

She let her breath out a moment later when she saw Chief Mathews standing in the doorway.

"Oh thank God," she said. "You scared me."

Mathews smiled sadly.

"I'm sorry about this, Ashley," he said.

And unbelievably, he moved towards her. She started to cry out but he grabbed hold of her, clamping his hand over her mouth.

Ashley started to struggle, just as she had out on the ocean, when the red devils had attacked, but then she felt the sting of a needle as it slid into her arm.

Her struggles ceased as the world faded and went black.

CHAPTER 21

After dropping Ashley off at her house, Travis went to meet Professor Spencer at his lab. He had already sent over a text a couple of hours earlier, detailing what had happened to Brody.

He hadn't yet heard from Lieutenant Collins, who was likely making phone calls – to Mayor Vernon, but more importantly, to the State Police and most probably the Feds.

Travis wondered if Mason would attempt a private salvage. All indications were that the main wreck had gone over the edge of the drop-off, into the deep-water canyons beyond, and the bulk of his shipment had most likely gone with it. If that was the case, Mason might find himself stymied, because there was no easy way to get at it without specialized deep-sea equipment.

On the other hand, it was possible he might want to tidy-up what was left behind on the upper shelf. Ashley had described several packets of white powder lying scattered about – certainly incriminating enough.

But it wasn't Travis' job to worry about that. He was perfectly willing to let the authorities deal with Colin Mason. As a private citizen, the last thing he wanted was to be involved. One-on-one, Travis was comfortable hand-to-hand with almost any man. Mason's goons had likely been trained by someone like himself. But Travis didn't have the backing of the special forces behind him anymore and Mason had money and connections.

Travis wondered if Ashley would be safe. He found himself taking a personal interest there. But he had to recognize that was likewise up to the professionals – if she was genuinely in danger, they were in the best position to protect her.

He sighed. When Brody had taken her down on that dive, that damn kid hadn't just gotten himself killed, but he'd put a lot of other people at risk – possibly even himself.

But wasn't that always the way of it? One thing always led to another. Historically, Travis believed most major world-events were more or less the consequence of bad decisions.

When he arrived at the lab, he found Clyde sitting at his computer desk, updating his personal files. He glanced up as Travis walked in.

"I've been watching the news," Clyde said. "They haven't mentioned the incident today."

Travis nodded.

"I'm sure Collins is keeping things close to the vest for the moment."

He looked over Spencer's shoulder. The professor was typing up Travis' own description of Brody's attack.

"You aren't posting that on the site yet, are you?"

Clyde shook his head.

"Not yet. We'll wait until it's public knowledge."

Spencer removed his glasses, turning in his chair.

"You're certain this young man was killed by the Colossals? Not the Humboldts?"

"I didn't actually see anything myself. I got there after the fact. But they were there. And I've got several witnesses to the attack, including one who saw it up-close and personal."

"Well then," Clyde said, "we can update our behavior-profile on *Mesonychoteuthis*. I think we can safely say at least one of our long-term questions about Colossal squid behavior has been conclusively answered."

Travis nodded. "And not in a good way."

"It's ironic," Clyde continued. "Before we even knew about Colossals, the giant squid was already famously one of the most elusive large predators on the planet. But the Colossal squid is more than three times its mass, and we know dramatically less about it."

Travis knew that Clyde was thinking like a scientist, examining possibilities and variables based on new information. It was the sort of thing that might have come across as cold-blooded, considering that a young man had died, but Travis understood that the emotional separation was a necessity. Clyde had a personal stake. Emotion was not absent here, but buried, and had been ever since the death of his own father, at the hands – or tentacles – of the same monstrous beast.

A scientist was always frustrated to be reduced to secondhand information. There were so many unknown factors when you were without direct observation of a living Colossal. The only option was to base conjecture on what was known about related species.

But even though *Architeuthis* was nearest in size to *Mesonychoteuthis* and they were both squid, the two species actually didn't really resemble each other all that much. A giant squid, by all indications, was a solitary hunter. It was also a long, narrow-bodied animal. And in the way that form fitted function, one could assume a behavior that befitted that slender, graceful design. That also affected temperament.

An animal's temperament was a factor that couldn't be overstated. Habits of giant squid were not well-known, but just by looking at them, you could tell they were not built for the sort of Hail-Mary assaults characteristic of their smaller red devil cousins.

But Colossals on the other hand, were built a lot more like Humboldts. In fact, size notwithstanding, they were actually *more* heavily built, and pound-for-pound, they were much more powerfully armed. They had the appearance of a feisty animal.

What had happened today certainly supported that.

There were also other important considerations.

"Up until now," Clyde said, "we could safely assume that *Mesonychoteuthis* would reproduce in the same high-numbers that all squid species do, which would also mean they are potentially subject to the same sort of sudden bursts in population during high-survival years.

"But," he continued, "in the case of Colossals, I've long suspected that these population booms are directly tied to the movements of the Humboldt squid. The appearances of the larger species may bisect centuries as opposed to years or decades, but the evidence suggests that they always follow the Humboldts."

Spencer nodded affirmatively.

"Sometimes the Humboldts are there without them, but they always follow the Humboldts." He shrugged. "I can only speculate as to why, but they do. And the longer timeline between appearances may simply be that the sheer weight of biomass slows down the life-cycle. But here they are."

"The attack on the young man today," Clyde said, "if it really played out as described, is also the first evidence that these larger animals will swarm and mob prey, just like the Humboldts do."

Travis ran his fingers over his old Humboldt scars, trying to imagine a similar swarm of Colossals. They would tear something the size of a human being apart.

Would. *Had.* Ashley had seen it up close. He wondered what that would look like.

"We're going to be asked our opinion by the local authorities on how to handle it," Travis said. "What do we do?"

Clyde shrugged.

"Honestly? Nothing. It's like so much in nature. People think that just because humans can sometimes affect nature that we can control it. Even regulate it. Nothing could be further from the truth."

Spencer shook his head.

"This isn't like some rogue animal that can be fished out, or even a normal population that can be culled by standard fishing methods. These animals live deep down. What they do is up to them, not us. They may just be passing through, or they may decide to stay a while. All we can do is just wait and see."

Travis sighed.

"You're basically saying these waters are not going to be safe until, when-and-if, they decide to leave on their own. Mayor Vernon isn't going to like hearing that."

"Whatever brought these creatures here is beyond our control," Clyde replied, "and when it's time, they will likely move on. Just as the Humboldts do. And my guess is that we won't see them again for the better part of a century.

"Of course," he allowed, "I could be wrong. When push comes to shove, I'm just guessing. And while it may be as educated a guess as possible, it's still based on extremely limited knowledge."

At that moment, Travis' phone rang. He glanced down at his flashing screen. There was no number, and he normally didn't answer blank calls, but he was waiting on word from both Ashley and Collins.

But as he pressed receive, a video screen popped up and he recognized the smiling face of Colin Mason.

"Mr. Prescott," Mason greeted amiably, "how are you this evening?"

Travis frowned. His eyes turned grimly to Clyde. He turned his phone to keep the professor out of the view.

"Mr. Mason," Travis replied. "What's the occasion?"

"Well, I was actually looking for your help. I have a bit of a dilemma that I think you are just the person to help me with."

"What's that?"

"Well, as you know, I had a boat go down in the deep water beyond the drop-off, and it was carrying a valuable cargo that I would very much like to recover. Normally, I would just handle the salvage operation myself, but as it turns out, this particular terrain requires specialized equipment that is not easy to come by on short notice."

"I also understand," Mason said, "that you have at your disposal, a deep-water submersible that would be perfect for the task."

Travis shook his head politely.

"I'm sorry, Mr. Mason. I don't hire-out for that kind of work." Travis smiled. "Insurance issues."

Mason smiled back thinly.

"Of course," he said. "Unfortunately, time is of the essence, so I really must insist."

Travis shook his head again.

"I'm afraid not."

Mason was nodding agreeably.

"I thought you might say that," he said. "I would, however, ask you to consider this."

Mason turned his phone screen to one side.

Lying on the couch beside him was Ashley. She appeared unconscious.

Travis let out a slow breath.

"Mr. Mason, if you've hurt her...," he began.

"I assure you, she's fine," Mason said. "For the moment. Just sleeping off a mild sedative. She should be coming around soon. But I certainly hope you are here when she does."

"Mr. Mason," Travis said, "I really have to tell you, I'm more inclined to call the police."

"Yes," Mason said. "I'm sure."

Now he turned his camera to where Chief Mathews was standing beside him. Mathews looked back at the screen unhappily, but resolute.

"I have a lot of employees, Mr. Prescott," Mason said.

Travis said nothing.

"I'll see you out at the drop-off site in one hour, then?" Mason said brightly. "Please don't disappoint me."

The Cheshire cat smile seemed to hover briefly on Travis' screen as Mason clicked off.

Travis put his phone back in his pocket. Mason had just provided him information that he knew he couldn't be allowed to live with. He turned a grim eye to Spencer.

"You realize both our lives are no longer worth a dime," he said. "Colin Mason isn't the type to leave loose-ends. Once this is done, we'll both disappear."

"What are you going to do?" Clyde asked.

Travis considered.

"Well," he said, "I guess there's really no choice."

He pulled his keys from his pocket. The boat was at the dock. The submersible was locked away in the boathouse. It would take some time to set up. And he was on the clock.

Then he turned to the locked safe in the corner, tapping out the combination. Inside was a nine-millimeter semi-automatic and several packs of ammo. Travis pulled out the pistol and slapped a cartridge into the chamber. His eyes turned grimly back to Clyde.

"I'm headed out there," he said.

CHAPTER 22

Ashley came back to consciousness slowly. The effects of the drug were like anesthetic and she blinked groggily. Her brain registered the glare of overhead lights as she finally came awake.

She looked around, confused, not quite immediately able to recall what had happened or how she might have got there, like the blackout period after a hangover.

Then she saw Colin Mason, sitting in his chair, sipping at a glass of wine and watching her.

Ashley sat bolt-upright, a surge of ice-water pumping through her veins, shocking her back to full awareness.

Mason smiled.

"Nice to see you awake, Miss Wells," he said.

Ashley looked around the room, and realized she was sitting aboard Mason's yacht.

The luxury on display was as deliberate as it was decadent. The chamber was split into two levels, with a wheelchair-friendly access ramp instead of stairs. There was a bar and tables up top, and lounge furniture spread out on the lower floor. Large TV screens hung from the ceilings in every corner, in the manner of a sport's restaurant, with one large screen dominating the middle of the room.

Mason sipped at his wine as he hit the lever on his chair, moving closer.

"I apologize for the circumstances, Miss Wells," he said, "but I thought it possible you might decline an invitation. And I am rather pressed for time."

"What am I doing here?" Ashley asked.

As she spoke, she heard the tremor in her own voice, as her mind was already contemplating the possibilities.

"Several reasons, actually," Mason said. "For one, it has come to my attention that you were not completely honest with me when we talked this afternoon. Chief Mathews tells me that you saw a little more than wreckage down on the sea floor today."

Ashley blinked as the effects of the drug faded, and she remembered Chief Mathews standing at her door, coming at her with the needle.

Mason eyed her seriously.

"I understand the circumstances were stressful," he said, "but I must insist on complete candor from you from this point on. Are we agreed?"

Mason picked up a remote from the table.

"We are currently anchored just before the drop-off. Let me show you what's out there right now."

He clicked the remote and the TV screens all turned on at once.

The images that came alive were of schooling fish and the now-familiar blinking red arrow-shapes moving among them. The boat lights illuminated the water surrounding the yacht as the cameras recorded the nightly feeding of the Humboldts.

"This seems to be the particular canyon where they've been congregating," Mason said. "They really are fascinating creatures. Quite beautiful in their own way, don't you think?"

Mason watched the screens for a moment as if mesmerized.

"It's actually remarkable that I was never really aware of them before," he said. "I've always had an affinity for ocean predators."

He grinned meaningfully as he tapped his hip just above his missing leg. "Of course, until now, my primary interest has always been in sharks. Great Whites, in particular. But they are unfortunately not much in evidence this year."

Mason turned back to Ashley.

"But nature abhors a vacuum. Remove one alpha predator, and another will rise to take its place."

"Why did you bring me here?" Ashley asked again.

"Well," Mason replied, "you are my own little insurance policy. You see, I am a very careful man. Experience has taught me to be." He again patted the empty space of his missing leg. "And one of the primary requirements for a man in my position is an understanding of risk management. Determining the safest course of action to conduct business. As does any responsible entrepreneur.

"Right now," he said, "I have an expensive cargo that I'm trying to recover. But two problems have developed. The first is the depth at which it currently resides, which is beyond the reach of conventional divers."

Mason turned to the screen, indicating the schooling Humboldts chasing their nightly meal.

"This," he said, "is the second. Fascinating as I may find them, they are a rather formidable obstacle."

"I don't see any of the big ones," Ashley said.

Mason nodded.

"I have no doubt that they are out there," he said. "According to your friend, Mr. Prescott's colleague, Professor Spencer, the larger squid follow the path of the smaller ones. I assume you have you seen their site? *Release the Kraken*? It is very informative.

"But," he continued, turning back to Ashley, "whether they are or not, in either case, it is simply not practical to attempt a recovery salvage with divers." Mason indicated the wounds on Ashley's own arms. "Even the smaller ones have proven to be quite aggressive and dangerous. Something to which you have direct experience. And that's not to mention what happened to your friend Brody."

Ashley shuddered.

"What are you going to do with me?" she asked.

"Well," Mason said, smiling easily, "that depends on what your Mr. Prescott can do for *me*. You see, Mr. Prescott is something of a specialist in deep-water operations. And more importantly, he has access to a submersible that can facilitate my salvage. And I am always generous to people who do me favors.

"So," he said, "I have requested that Mr. Prescott meet us out here tonight. That was about forty-five minutes ago. If he shows, we will perform our salvage. And depending upon how that goes, we will move forward from there."

Mason took a sip of wine.

"In the meantime," he said, "we have a little time to kill."

Mason stood from his wheelchair up on his one leg and hopped over to sit down beside her on the sofa. Ashley shrank back.

"Here," Mason said, pouring a second glass of wine and handing it to her. "Make yourself comfortable."

Ashley took the glass tentatively. The hungry look in Mason's eyes caused her to wonder if she might not be molested while they waited.

She needn't have worried. Mason had something else in mind.

He reached again for the remote, tapped a button and pointed it towards the large screen in the center of the room.

"You might remember Lindsey," Mason said. "My lady-friend from this afternoon."

He shook his head, his expression long-suffering.

"I'm afraid she suffered a little accident. My cameras managed to catch her last moments for posterity."

When the video came on, Ashley turned away in horror – only to have Mason's hand grab her by the hair and turn her roughly back towards the screen, forcing her to watch. His grip was like iron.

The image on the screen was beyond vile – for nothing else but the simple *fact* of it.

Ashley had seen what happened to Brody up close and personal, but this was murder.

Mason fell silent for a moment as his eyes devoured the images like the most proactive bit of pornography.

Tears began to stream down Ashley's cheeks as the images burned into her eyes.

She remembered the look in the young woman's eyes this afternoon – fear and sympathy – and deliberate distance – the look of a resigned slave.

Ashley had known Mason was a bad guy, but she never suspected he was *this* crazy.

But when he spoke, Mason's voice was as easy and congenial as ever.

"I hope," he said, "that this impresses upon you how important it is that you are completely honest with me from this point forward. And how vital it is that your Mr. Prescott shows up in a timely fashion."

But even as he said it, there came the sound of an approaching boat motor.

A moment later, one of Mason's goons – the bear-fellow, Leroy, who had pulled her from the water – poked his head in the lounge.

"Mr. Mason? He's here."

CHAPTER 23

Travis pulled up beside Mason's yacht, with the submersible in tow. Four of Mason's merc-goons stared down robotically from the railing.

He stepped out onto the floating dock and tied-off his mooring line. When he climbed up the small ladder up on deck, he immediately found four guns drawn on him.

Travis looked each man in the eye, looking for any sign of independent thought, and saw none.

"Stand-down, Leroy," a voice said from behind them. "I don't think that's necessary. Mr. Prescott is here to help us."

The largest of the goons, the same hairy bear-like gentleman Travis remembered from that afternoon, glanced over his shoulder, but nodded to the others, who all holstered their weapons. The group of them parted to reveal Mason sitting in his chair.

"I apologize, Mr. Prescott," Mason said. "My men are protective. Of course, I realize a man with your background isn't going to be intimidated by guns."

Mason smiled.

"Different strokes for different folks. In order to get people to do what you need them to, you have to understand how to appeal to them in a way that's effective. And for a man like you, *this* is what works."

Mason snapped his fingers.

"Chief Mathews," he said. "If you please."

The door to the yacht's lounge opened and Mathews appeared. He was holding Ashley by one arm, leading her out on deck.

Travis' eyes narrowed at Mathews, who looked unhappy, but didn't drop his eyes, instead, he pulled out his service pistol and pressed it against Ashley's head.

Ashley's face was wet with tears.

"I'm sorry, Travis," she said.

"It's not your fault, honey," Travis said. He thought about saying something like, 'It's going to be okay', but he wasn't one for making false promises.

Mason smiled.

"Not to be rude," he said, "but I'm going to ask Leroy here to frisk you real quick. Just a formality, considering the circumstances."

Travis raised his hands accommodatingly, allowing Leroy to pat him down. He had come dressed in cargo shorts, a light jacket and a t-shirt, hiding nothing.

Leroy looked over at Mason. "Nothing, boss."

"No guns, no knives," Mason said. "I'm almost insulted."

"Don't be," Travis replied. "I don't need a gun or a knife." He glanced at Leroy. "Not for *these* guys."

Leroy glared back menacingly.

Mason's smile widened.

"Of course. Well then, Mr. Prescott. Shall we get to it?"

Mason rolled his chair over to the railing, looking down at the water. Schooling Humboldts moved in and out of the boat-lights under the yacht as they fed, careless of the humans prattling about above the surface.

"What kind of load are we talking about?" Travis asked.

"Roughly a ton. I'm hoping to recover at least the bulk of that."

Mason nodded to Leroy, who produced a container of nylon-fiber nets, equipped with metal frames.

"This is what we've used in similar cases in the past. Once we find the shipment, you load up each bag, hit the auto-inflate, and the container will be brought to the surface. Sort of like the catch-bags used in abalone-diving. Can your submersible's automated arm handle that?"

Travis nodded. "That shouldn't be a problem."

"Each container is designed to carry roughly five-hundred pounds. So four loads or less, depending on what's salvageable." Mason shrugged. "So this should be short and sweet."

"Except for the two-thousand foot dive," Travis replied.

"Well," Mason said amiably, "that's why we have you."

Travis didn't bother to ask what happened afterwards.

Leroy sat the container of catch-bags on the deck. Travis grabbed them up, hopped down the ladder and set about attaching them to the submersible's frame, within reach of the automated arm. It would take some working to manipulate them underwater, but he'd done similar operations in the past.

When he turned, he found Mason himself hopping down the ladder on his one leg, onto the floating dock beside him. He smiled, tapping a GoPro camera on his forehead.

"I'm going to want to get this on video," Mason said.

"What are you talking about?"

"I'm going down there with you," Mason replied. "I wouldn't miss this."

Travis pulled open the capsule to the sub.

"It's going to be crowded."

Mason nodded agreeably.

"Just so you know," Mason said, "if you should try anything untoward while we are down there... well, I'll just let you use your imagination as to what will happen to Miss Wells here."

Travis looked up at Ashley, standing there mutely, with Mathews' gun pressed against her temple.

"It's also worth mentioning," Mason added, "that *I* don't need a gun either."

Travis nodded. "Understood."

He motioned to the open portal to the submersible.

"After you."

With deceptive agility, Mason threw his one leg over into the hatch and clambered down into the capsule.

Travis spared one last look up at Ashley.

"Be brave, girl," he said.

Ashley shut her eyes, but nodded back.

Travis climbed down into the submersible.

Mason was a big man, despite his missing leg, but he made an effort to pack himself unobtrusively to the rear, giving Travis free access to the controls. He attached another camera to the front window, smiling broadly. He seemed in terribly good humor.

"Shall we?" he said brightly.

Mason signaled Leroy, who tossed the mooring rope clear, allowing the sub to drift away from the yacht. Travis started up the motor.

The submersible hung right at the waterline and they could see below the surface where the surrounding water was lit-up by the boat-lights under the yacht. The silvery bait-fish flashed past, chased by the red-blinking arrow-shapes of the Humboldts as they zipped back-and-forth, some of them veering in close as they zoomed by to check out this strange new object invading their territory.

Travis wondered if any of them recognized him from before.

He nodded to Mason, who was positively beaming.

"Ready?"

Mason's grin was like a kid's.

"Absolutely," he said.

Travis pulled the lever and the water bubbled as they dropped below the surface and began to descend.

CHAPTER 24

They dropped down into the darkness of the abyss.

Around them, the Humboldts circled.

Travis took the submersible straight down, quickly reaching the bottom of the shelf ahead of the drop-off. He switched his spotlight on, aiming it down onto the rocky floor.

Both fish and squid were schooling thickly together, and the view was like driving through a snow storm, the red and silver bodies reflected back, obstructing their vision. But they could still see the left-over bits of wreckage scattered about. The boat had apparently impacted on the shelf before the current had taken it over the cliff.

Among the wreckage, there were several packets of white powder.

"Is that what we're after?" Travis asked.

Mason nodded.

"Hopefully the bulk of the cargo's still with the boat."

The drop-off was just ahead. Travis sailed them over the edge, and there was a brief moment of free-fall right before they began to descend – hovered, perched, like a diver cresting, just as they began to fall.

Even with Mason by his side, even with the deadly circumstances, Travis still felt the rush, as they plunged into the dark depths, surrounded by a bubble of glass.

Beside him, Mason seemed utterly rapt.

"Never been in one of these before?" Travis asked.

"I never thought of it," Mason replied. "But now I'm thinking of buying one."

Travis nodded. Mason had a bizarre way about him – despite everything, he managed to come across as perversely likable. Travis supposed it wasn't all that unusual. In the special forces, he had been friends with people who had a taste for killing before. But he also understood the difference between personality and character. A lot of serial killers were known to be charming when you met them. That was part of their lure. Travis had no trouble resisting it.

The Humboldts continued to circle as they dropped ever deeper. Travis was actually surprised – he had expected most of them to be up feeding at the surface, but tonight that didn't seem to be the case. Perhaps the population boom was even greater than they had thought, because the ocean seemed filled with them, a virtual cloud of darting bio-luminescent arrow-shapes that, as they continued down, were now showing more interest in the glowing submersible. Their goggle eyes perked on top of their body mantels, regarding these strange surface creatures in that oddly curious manner.

But Travis reminded himself that there was only one reason for their interest.

In that way, they weren't all that different from Mason himself.

"How much further down?" Mason asked.

Travis checked his depth gauge.

"We're reaching fifteen-hundred feet now," he said. "The canyon bottoms out here at about two-thousand feet. But it gets even deeper out further. There's a secondary shelf that extends just past the drop-off. If your boat got taken into one of those, you might be out of luck."

Mason nodded.

"Can this submersible take us down that far?"

Travis shrugged.

"It can, but we still have to make it back up. We're on a limited charge, and a finite supply of oxygen. With two of us in here, we're going to be using up both a lot faster than normal. We'll have to keep an eye on our gauges."

As they dropped down alongside the canyon wall, the bottom now came into view. Travis aimed his spotlight along the floor.

Framed in the circle of light was the overturned hull of the wrecked boat.

Mason smiled.

"Score," he said.

Travis steered the submersible in that direction.

The Humboldts were circling closer now. At this depth, there were no bait-fish, but the red devils schooled around the wreck like sea-monsters guarding an old pirate treasure – which, Travis thought, was not far from what it actually was.

But the image was fantastical – a romanticism. This was very real.

And the Humboldts were not the only things down here.

Travis reminded himself of what else dwelled down here in this darkness, hiding in this permanent night, that even now probably lurked somewhere not far distant, just out of sight – no doubt watching and aware.

He realized he was afraid.

CHAPTER 25

Travis circled the submersible around the sunken wreck, shining his spotlight on the overturned hull.

The frame was broken open – probably from a combination of the initial impact with the floor of the upper shelf, before being dragged over the cliff by the current, and then the secondary impact with the canyon floor.

He aimed his spotlight along the stern, which they could now see boasted a gaping hole where the missing motor had been.

Ashley had told them she'd seen the motor lying loose on the shelf floor up above, adorned with claw marks. The fact that it was so far separate from the other wreckage implied that it must have been torn away before the rest of the boat sank.

The remaining frame around the stern looked like it had been raked by the claws of a grizzly bear.

"I'd say we have our mystery solved," Travis said.

"You think a Colossal did that?"

Travis nodded. "I do."

"Amazing," Mason said, as if in approval. He peered through the clear bubble, trying to see in the darkness. "You think they're still around?"

Travis nodded again.

"I do," he said. "If they really are following the Humboldts, they'll be around." He glanced up towards the far-distant surface. "I was thinking they might follow the little guys up top, but there's so many of them down here, there might not be any need."

Travis shook his head. This really *was* a population explosion. The Humboldts were schooling as thick down here as they were at the surface.

Mason turned his attention back to business.

"What about the cargo?" he asked.

Travis turned his light into the shattered hull. They could see the bags of power inside, still mostly safely packed.

Mason nodded.

"Shall we get to it?"

Moving the sub into position above the opening, Travis set the automated arm to work.

He proceeded deliberately, one movement at a time. The first job was to disengage the catch-bags – more difficult than it sounded with only one arm, despite the gripping claw. Travis had broken his arm once, in a high school wrestling match – it was back during the era of the button-down fly and he remembered trying to button-up his pants one-handed in the restroom – a laborious procedure that had taken several embarrassing minutes the first time he'd tried it. This was sort of like that.

Finally, he managed to free the container and pulled out the first of the loose nets, setting it on the sea floor beside the wreck, ready to be filled.

Mason watched the operation like an avid student, absorbing every movement, studying the controls and every measured action, while sitting obligingly aside and letting Travis work.

The Humboldts continued to circle curiously as Travis retrieved the first of the bags of powder, backing the submersible from the shattered hull.

But the moment the arm brought the white bag into the open, one of the red devils came darting out of the darkness, grasping onto the exposed bag, tearing it open, and spreading the white powder into the current.

Travis cursed under his breath.

"Well," Mason said. "That was about fifty-thousand dollars."

Travis tried again, and this time two of them darted in, attacking the package before it got anywhere near the catch-bag.

"Why, you little bastards," Mason marveled.

Travis frowned. "They seem to like this stuff."

"I buy quality," Mason said. "What do we do about it?"

"Actually," Travis replied, "I'm not sure. I suppose we could keep trying until they figure out it's not food. But that might not even be it. They're known to treat unfamiliar objects aggressively. They might just keep attacking."

He checked his meters, shaking his head.

"But we don't have forever," he said. "We're going to have to surface before too long."

"Well," Mason said, "this is your job. Get it done."

His affected amiable tone was replaced by steely command. Travis glanced at him, feeling a little spark of temper, and fought it off immediately. A cool head was paramount if you were underwater ten feet, and they were down well over two-thousand.

"Well," he said, considering, "I guess we could try putting the catch-bag in the hull, and loading it in there. But it still has to get to the surface, and if they're going after the individual packets, they may go for the catch-bags too."

Mason nodded neutrally, still willing to defer. Travis was the expert, and Mason was prepared to allow him to fail or succeed on his own merits – the consequences of failure to be determined later on.

Travis adjusted the arm, grabbing up another catch-bag and setting it inside the broken hull. Within the confines of the wreck, the movements were more labored, but he was at least able to fill the bag.

He wondered what his donors would say if they knew their expensive undersea submersible would one day be used as a tool for drug packing.

It was, however, all taking longer than planned. The estimate of four loads seemed about accurate, but it was in no way going to be short and sweet. Soon they were going to have to surface.

Finally, he was able to get the first load filled. He grabbed up the catch-bag and backed the sub out of the hull.

"Okay," he said, "let's see what they do."

He activated the automatic inflation float and let the container go. It rose like a balloon, ascending quickly for the surface.

The Humboldts circled, but for the moment, seemed to be letting it go unmolested.

Then Travis saw a flash of movement from behind them – something large that had been waiting just at the periphery, like a lion skulking just outside the light of a campfire in the jungle.

The mass that came lunging out of the darkness flashed fire-engine red, and was easily the size of the submersible itself. Travis saw two twenty-foot tentacles stretching out, latching onto the catch-bag, pulling it back into a squirming mass of eight grasping arms, each lined with talons and thick as a man's leg, and then into the melon-sized beak.

Mason blurted a startled curse.

Suddenly, the larger shapes were circling all around them, emboldened, and moving in.

Travis whistled through his teeth.

"I think we're in trouble," he said.

CHAPTER 26

The beast tore the five-hundred-pound catch-bag apart like a feather pillow and the billowing cloud of powder was quickly swept away.

Travis had time to wonder how much *that* little white cloud was worth before the submersible was rocked by a heavy impact.

Tentacles wrapped around the clear acrylic glass, and they could see the clawing talons, so viciously different, even from the nasty, edged suckers that lined the arms of the red devils, as they searched for purchase. Pressed against the window was a massive beak, that yawned and snapped, hunting for a weak spot.

"Jesus," Mason whispered. "Can it get in here?"

"Probably not through the glass," Travis said. "That's acrylic sapphire. Damn near diamond. But if we give it enough time, it might figure out how to open the portal. These are smart animals. An octopus in a tank can screw open a jar to get at a crab. And that beak is like a wire cutter. Not that it really matters. If it keeps us down here, we'll run out of air before that happens."

Travis tried the motor, which whirred noisily, but the sub wouldn't budge.

There was a second impact, this time from behind, as a second beast latched on.

"What do we do?" Mason said, eyes wide.

Travis was pleased for just a moment to see Mason actually looking scared.

Not that *he* wasn't.

Travis pressed the specially-designed button on the console, and the electric blue flash lit up the water.

Outside, the giant tentacles jerked spasmodically and released.

"Well," Travis said, "that worked. For the moment, anyway. Unfortunately, we have a limited charge and our power is already starting to run low."

He glanced at Mason.

"How much is that cargo worth to you now, Mr. Mason?"

Mason looked around at the massive shapes still circling. The Colossals were chasing the schooling Humboldts that seemed oblivious to the predation, and they continued to circle the sunken wreck as the larger squid picked them off, one at a time.

"Get us the hell out of here," Mason said.

Travis nodded, for the first time in full-agreement. He hit the propulsion lever.

But the submersible did not get twenty-feet before it was attacked again – three of them this time, mobbing the sub exactly as Travis had seen Humboldts swarm another squid on a jig-hook. The two men were shaken inside the glass globe like dice. Another electric charge sent the massive beasts skirting, but this time the lights on the console dimmed briefly.

"Ahhhh *shit*," Travis muttered.

"Get us out of here, Prescott," Mason said, his voice again reverting to terse command.

Travis felt another spark of temper, but took a breath, trying to think.

Then his eyes happened on the container of catch-bags still clinging to the sub's frame. He turned the automated arm, grabbing one of them up.

"What are you doing?" Mason asked.

"Giving them something to chase besides us," Travis replied.

He set the auto-inflate and the bag went scooting for the surface. It rose like a balloon, faster than before, unhampered by the weight.

Immediately, the squid pursued, lunging at the fleeing catch-bag and tearing it to shreds.

Travis let another one go, and then one more for good measure, as each was set-upon and torn apart.

Next, he shut off all the submersible's lights. The clearing on the canyon floor was suddenly enveloped in total inky blackness.

But they could still see circling squid of all sizes, a constantly-moving kaleidoscope of bio-luminescent light.

It really would have been quite beautiful if it wasn't so savage.

Travis hit the lever and the sub began to rise.

The buzz of the motor belied the sense of stasis, as if instead of moving, they were hanging completely still in the darkness. The only point of reference were the glowing bodies of the circling squid.

Something bumped the submersible from behind and Travis saw a massive shape speeding away, flashing red.

"They're attracted to light, but they still know we're here."

"How does this thing test for impact?" Mason asked.

Travis shrugged.

"Actually, I don't really know. It's designed to resist pressure, but that's not exactly the same thing. It can't be good to take those hits. The glass is probably okay, but we've got lots of moving parts."

Travis started to release another catch-bag, but this time, as he extended the automatic arm to release it, they were hit directly from the front.

The squid ignored the bag, perhaps growing wise, and latched onto the submersible itself. These beasts were smart. It knew *this* was the thing that was moving. And in the dark, the sensitive bulbous eyes – largest in the animal kingdom – no doubt detected even the faint glow of the lights on the console.

Now there was a series of heavy impacts as they were once again mobbed.

"Prescott..." Mason began nervously.

Travis hit the electric charge. The blue current of energy channeled through the water and the tentacles released. But a bare moment later, they were hit once more. Travis turned on the lights, illuminating a massive beast clinging to the automated arm.

"Is that thing looking at us?" Mason asked.

"I think it is."

"The electric charge didn't bother it?"

"Oh, I think it did. I think it pissed it off, and now it wants to fight."

Travis wondered how big the thing was. There were only a few complete specimens of Colossal squid that had ever been recovered, and even the largest of them were all juveniles. But beaks found inside the stomachs of sperm whales implied animals approaching a ton. And this beast looked easily that. The beak that scraped the glass was bigger than any Travis had ever seen. And this was just *one* of them.

He took a moment to regard Mason's blinking camera still attached to the dash, recording it all. Half-bemused, he realized this would be the first footage ever taken of an adult Colossal in its own environment. Clyde would have *loved* it.

Travis hit the electric charge again, this time holding the lever down.

For a long moment, the squid hung stubbornly, but finally released.

Within the submersible, there was a loud spark and the sudden smell of ozone.

The lights blinked off as the power cut out, and they were left sitting in darkness.

"Well," Travis said, "that might have screwed us."

Mason reached into his pocket and pulled out his phone.

"What are you doing?" Travis asked.

"I'm letting my men know we're in trouble," Mason replied. Travis smirked.

"What exactly do you expect them to do?"

"I don't know, goddamn it. We have a winch on the boat. Maybe they can get a line down to us."

Travis laughed.

"We're still down almost fifteen-hundred feet. That would be like shooting in the dark."

"Well, we can't just sit here."

Mason pushed the call button. His screen sat on pause, waiting for a signal.

"The canyon wall might be blocking your signal," Travis said.

Mason swore, touching the button again.

Then the submersible shook once more.

The big one was already back – or maybe it was even another. The light of Mason's phone illuminated the clawed tentacles and chomping beak.

Travis felt the sub turning in the water as the beast began to drag them back down to the bottom.

CHAPTER 27

Ashley sat on the lounge couch, her legs curled up into a ball. Leroy and Chief Mathews both stood guard at the door. Mathews' face remained wooden, and he kept his eyes deliberately averted.

Then a ring-tone sounded. Leroy pulled his phone from his pocket and held it to his ear.

"Yeah, boss?"

Ashley could hear the broken contact of Mason's voice.

"Leroy... we're.... out of... need help..."

Then the call dropped. Leroy frowned and tapped the screen, attempting to call back, but got nothing.

After a moment, there was a ding of an incoming text.

Leroy's frown deepened.

"It says they're in trouble," he said. Another text beeped, but then that dropped as well. Leroy tapped his screen, trying to recover the message. Failing that, he turned to the door. He patted Mathews on the shoulder as he nodded to Ashley.

"Keep an eye on her," he said as he stepped outside, trying to raise a better signal.

When he had gone, Ashley looked up at Mathews.

"How can you do this?" she said.

Mathews' expression never changed.

"Sometimes," he said, "people don't have a choice."

Ashley eyed him coldly.

"Don't they?"

Mathews shrugged.

"Okay," he said, "sometimes you have a choice between two evils. I have a daughter your age. And once upon a time, I thought I was being a good cop and I busted a drug dealer who had connections to Colin Mason. And so my choice was to go on the payroll, or have happen to her something like what's going to happen to you."

His apathetic matter-of-fact tone was chilling.

"What's going to happen to me?" Ashley asked.

Now Mathews' eyes cast in her direction. Then he nodded to the series of view-screens, and the images of the schooling Humboldts that circled in and out of the boat-lights under the yacht.

"You saw the preview, didn't you?" he said grimly. "Mason has got a whole new game."

Ashley shut her eyes. The vile images of the video Mason had shown her were burned in her brain.

Mathews shook his head.

"The only difference between Colin Mason and a normal serial killer is that he's got the money and power to indulge it. I've been a cop for thirty years, and I've seen some pretty foul shit. You'd never believe what the average person will do in private if they think they can get away with it."

He seemed to repress a shudder.

"But for a guy like Mason, there's no accountability at all." Mathews regarded Ashley. "Take that away and what might *you* do?"

Ashley looked right back.

"Not *this*."

Mathews smiled cynically.

"Neither would I. But I've *got* accountability. And I've chosen my evil."

They heard activity outside, and Leroy shouting at the others.

Mathews nodded.

"They're in trouble down there," he said. "With any luck, God will do us all a favor and that son of a bitch will stay down there forever."

"Travis is down there too," Ashley said.

Mathews shook his head.

"Trust me, girl. It would be worth it. And if Prescott knew half of what I know about Colin Mason, he'd think so too."

"And what happens to me then? Does that mean I get to go free?"

Mathews was silent a moment, and Ashley thought she saw a flutter of regret. But then the wooden expression fell over his face once again.

"Well," he said, "maybe you won't be eaten alive."

He turned away, looking out the window at the ocean beyond.

"Lesser of two evils," he said.

CHAPTER 28

Outside the yacht, Travis' boat rocked with the waves, bumping up against the floating dock.

Inside the cabin, the couch seat flipped over and Professor Clyde Spencer sat up out of the storage compartment beneath. In his hand, he held Travis' nine-millimeter.

Cautiously, he climbed out onto the dock. It wasn't as dark as he'd hoped. The water below was illuminated by the boat-lights and the yacht itself was adorned with spotlights.

He could hear Mason's goons shouting back and forth, and as he made his way up the ladder onto the main deck, he caught snippets of their conversation. From what he could gather, the submersible was in some kind of trouble.

Clyde cursed silently. He knew Travis was a specialist in this kind of operation, but the circumstances were unprecedented.

But there was nothing he could do. Travis was on his own. Clyde had his own job to do. He set his teeth, keeping as best he could to the shadows, while he crept along the deck to get a look at what he had waiting for him.

He could see four of them, milling about the back of the boat, looking over the side. All of them big, all carrying sidearms.

For a moment, Clyde considered simply opening fire. He was pretty sure he could drop at least two of them before the others reacted. On the other hand, there might be more of them, and after those first two, the others would no doubt start shooting back.

Not yet, he decided. He sat back, listening.

"Exactly what the hell does Mason expect us to do?" one of the men was saying.

"I couldn't tell," another answered, a big burly fellow who seemed to be in charge. "I think he said something about using the winch."

"Are you kidding, Leroy?" the first man balked. "Why not just drop a fishing line with a bobber?"

"We've got diving gear on board," another man suggested.

But Leroy was shaking his head.

"We don't know how deep they are. They were headed to the canyon bottom. They might be down fifteen-hundred feet or more. You can't dive that far."

The first man gestured over the side.

"Even if you could, look at it down there. You want to get in the water with *that*?"

Over the side, the schooling Humboldts were still busy with their nightly feeding, skirting after the shoals of schooling fish, gliding in and out of range of the boat-lights.

That gave Clyde an idea.

Skulking back towards the cabin, he found the fuse box bolted outside the engine compartment. He found the switch for the underwater lights and switched them off, along with the lights along the side deck.

"What the hell?" came Leroy's voice. "Did we blow a fuse?"

"I'll get it," the first man said.

Clyde saw a shadow coming around the corner, and ducked out of sight in the now-accommodating darkness. A large barrel-chested man with bushy red hair and no neck appeared.

The man was muttering impatiently under his breath as he opened the fuse box, shining a penlight inside, hunting for the switch to turn the breakers back on.

As he did so, Clyde stepped up behind him and clubbed him with the pistol butt across the back of the head. The man dropped bonelessly to the deck.

Clyde was in his seventies, and he was no SEAL, but he'd been a Navy-man who'd done two tours in Vietnam – this wouldn't be the first man he'd killed hand-to-hand. With every bit of his strength, he raised the pistol and smacked the downed goon twice more, just to make sure the son of a bitch was dead, and then he kicked the spasming body through the railing overboard.

As the body hit the water, there was a sudden rush below the now-darkened surface and flashes of glowing arrow-shapes as the red devils came charging in after this new chunk of meat.

They were playing for keeps here.

Clyde turned back to the fuse-box and now he turned off the rest of the breakers. The lights cut out and the entire boat went dark.

He wiped the blood off the pistol butt as he stepped back into the shadows and waited.

CHAPTER 29

As Ashley sat with Mathews in the lounge, the surrounding view-screens suddenly went dark. The sets seemed to still be on and the image feed continued, but the boat-lights and the cameras under the yacht had apparently clicked off.

Mathews perked curiously, moving towards the window, looking outside.

A minute later, the lights in the lounge went off as well. Ashley sat up, blinking in the dark.

"What's happening?"

Mathews shook his head, pulling out his phone, and shining the screen light out the window.

"I don't know," he said. "Maybe they blew a circuit."

As he peered out the portal, they heard a mutter of commotion outside, and Leroy's voice shouting, "Oh, for crying out loud. Did that idiot crap-out the whole fuse-box?" And then louder, "Virgil! What the hell are you doing?"

It was eerily dark in the cabin. They were miles from shore and the darkness was like what you got out in the woods at night, with no ambient light except for the moon and stars above.

Then in the middle of that blackness, they heard gunshots – two at first, followed by shouts, and then four more shots in quick succession.

"What the hell?" Mathews pushed back quickly from the window-port, drawing his own gun and turning towards the door.

Ashley sat wide-eyed as the two of them listened in the suddenly deafening silence. They heard no more voices.

Shutting off the light on his phone, Mathews cautiously put his hand on the door latch. With his pistol aimed, he slowly pushed open the door, peering out onto the deck.

There was nothing. After a moment, he blinked his phone-light on again, scanning the area like a beat-cop shining a flashlight down an alley.

He glanced back at Ashley, then stepped back into the room, pulling the door shut behind him.

As he did so, the door was suddenly hit from behind. Mathews was knocked back, stumbling, his phone sent loose and flying, casting the room in spinning light.

In stop-motion flashes, Ashley saw Professor Clyde Spencer burst through the doorway. In his hand was a pistol, out and aimed.

Mathews cursed, regaining his footing, bringing his own gun up.

Without hesitation, Clyde Spencer fired. The explosions of simultaneous gunfire lit up the room in blinding flashes.

Mathews was knocked back with a guttural grunt, and he hit the floor.

Her vision mottled with after-glares, Ashley heard Mathews groan – she had the impression of him scrambling, and then raising his pistol once more.

Clyde fired again. The flash of the gun muzzle provided a snapshot image of Mathews' head snapping back as Spencer shot him between the eyes.

Mathews' body kicked once and lay still.

"Bastard," Clyde muttered.

He turned to Ashley, who was still sitting, wide-eyed and mute on the sofa.

"Are you alright?" he asked.

Ashley started to rise, still flash-blinded, her legs trembling, as Clyde reached out his hand.

But then the door behind him was suddenly thrown open again and Ashley saw a bulky frame fill the entranceway.

"How's this, you son of a bitch?" Leroy snarled. His shirt was bloody and he had his own pistol out and aimed.

There was another explosion of gunfire as Leroy fired blindly into the dark room. Ashley dived for cover and heard Clyde cry out in pain.

Spencer was down on the floor, and Leroy speared him with a flashlight. Ashley could see Clyde holding his leg. His pistol had been knocked clear.

Leroy was smiling as he raised his own gun again, leveled at Clyde's head.

Ashley stood, grabbing up Mason's bottle of expensive wine, and swung it across the back of Leroy's head. The bottle broke and the big man staggered, starting to turn towards her.

Looking down at the broken shard of the bottleneck in her hand, Ashley lunged forward and stuck the jagged glass into Leroy's throat.

Leroy gurgled, stumbling back. Reflexively, he reached for her, bringing his gun up at the same time.

With a wild, savage scream, Ashley stabbed out with the broken bottle, charging forward, even as Leroy's pistol fired, sending a bullet searing just past her face.

Ashley felt the spurt of warm blood as, this time, the jagged glass found the jugular. Leroy's knees buckled. Ashley stabbed again as the big man fell to the floor.

For a moment, Ashley stood there, staring down wide-eyed as Leroy struggled weakly. Then with another yell, she brought the broken bottleneck down again, in a fusillade of stabbing blows. Blood sprayed droplets in all directions, covering her face as she battened down, screaming louder with each impact.

A moment later, Clyde was beside her in the dark, grabbing hold of her. For just a second, she struggled in his arms, but then went utterly limp, dropping to her knees and crying.

"Easy girl," Clyde said, holding her close. "You're going to be alright."

They sat like that for several minutes, Ashley's heart hammering until the adrenaline passed. Finally, she looked up at Spencer in the dark, and he helped her to her feet.

Limping on his wounded leg, he led her up onto the main deck. She followed him around the main cabin, back to the still-open fuse-box, where he turned the yacht's power back on. The bright lights were momentarily as blinding as the dark.

When Ashley could see again, she looked around her, and lying on the deck were two more of Mason's men, both shot cleanly between the eyes.

Then Clyde looked out over the railing into the water. With the underwater lights back on, they could see the Humboldts still circling.

"What about Travis?" Ashley asked.

Clyde shook his head.

"I don't know yet," he said. He pulled out his phone and tapped a number.

Lieutenant Randy Collins' voice answered on the other end.

"Talk to me," Collins said.

"Come on in," Clyde replied.

CHAPTER 30

The Kraken was dragging them back down to the bottom.

Travis had ducked under the console and was trying to find the burnt fuses by the glow of a penlight in his teeth. The crowded space made it more difficult.

Mason had sent several texts to the surface, and had finally given up, simply sitting patiently, waiting for Travis to work.

Travis felt the beads of sweat dripping off his forehead. He took deliberate breaths, remembering his own council – all the years of field operations, which he'd tried to impress upon those he had trained himself.

Stay calm. Don't let the situation keep you from thinking intelligently *about* the situation.

But even as he worked, he realized that no matter if they got the power back on, the motor would never be able to get them to the surface with this creature hanging on. And if more of them joined in, they were as good as dead.

And while the beast didn't like that electric charge, it clearly wasn't enough to keep it away for long – and if they burned out the circuits a second time, they had no more replacements.

In the meantime, the submersible was being pulled right back down to the bottom of the canyon.

Mason was growing anxious.

"Any luck yet, Prescott?" he asked.

Travis had to hand it to him, Mason was remaining calm. The man was clearly used to pressure. Which, Travis supposed, shouldn't be surprising.

"I've almost got the circuits switched," he said. "But that's not going to get us out of the woods. This thing isn't going to let us go. And that electric charge isn't strong enough to keep it off for long."

But even as he said it, he had a sudden inspiration.

Sitting up quickly, he shouldered past Mason to the back of the sub. He started unscrewing the compartment to the motor.

"What are you doing?"

"Disconnecting the motor," Travis replied.

Mason blinked.

"Why exactly would you want to do that?"

"Because I have an idea."

Travis pulled the power cords, rerouting them under the console. He shoved the new fuses back into place and rebooted the system. There was a jolt and the interior lights came on.

Outside the sub, the squid reacted to the sudden flash. The tentacles squirmed, squeezing tighter, as if with a prey trying to escape.

Travis turned the automated arm and grabbed hold of the beast by the cusp of its mantle. The squid responded by latching on with several of its own arms. Travis clamped the grappling claw shut.

He glanced at Mason.

"Here goes nothing," he said and pressed the button on the console.

There was a sudden blinding flare in the water as the blue electric flash was replaced by a ball of pure white.

The squid recoiled, letting go its grip as it had done before. But this time, Travis didn't let go his, clinging with the grappling claw, and keeping his finger on the electric charge.

They were rocked as the beast started to struggle, tossing the submersible physically back and forth.

"Jesus," Mason said, "*look* at that thing."

The beast was flashing like an ambulance and blasting clouds of black ink as it tried to retreat.

Travis looked at the bulbous eyes staring at them through the window, and found it hard not to take it personally.

"How do you like *that*, you big ugly bastard?" he said, and kept his finger pressed on the button.

The lights in the sub started to flicker, but Travis held on. Outside, the squid was threatening to tear the automated arm loose.

But it was also beginning to cook.

And now its struggles were attracting its fellows.

As the other squid came swooping in, Travis released his grip, letting the half-fried beast pull away.

He had seen many Humboldts cannibalized by their own while struggling, trapped on a jig-line, and this was just like that. Massive fifteen-hundred and two-thousand pound bodies battened upon their hapless mate. The big Colossal battled and fought as the others began to eat it alive.

"My *God*," Mason whispered, awed.

But now their sub was floating without a motor and it would still take a few minutes to reroute the cables back.

Travis turned the automated arm to the remaining catch-bags. Looping the first one around the entry portal, he activated the auto-inflate. The submersible began to pull upright in the water. He attached two more, letting the bags shoot upwards like air-balloons, and then the sub began to slowly drift back up towards the surface.

Below, the half-fried chunk of still-struggling meat maintained a distraction as the submersible started to pull away.

Travis ducked back under the console, yanking out the wires, leaving them once again briefly in darkness, as he reattached the cables to the motor.

He hit reboot again and the lights came back on, and the buzz of the motor started-up right along with it.

Travis grabbed the controls and the craft began buzzing energetically back for the surface.

"I'll be damned," Mason said, regarding Travis. "I don't suppose you'd consider coming to work for me?"

Travis glanced at Mason sideways, actually suppressing an amazed chuckle.

"Well," he said, "first things first. Let's finish trying to stay alive."

Mason was still smiling as they at last began to draw near the surface. They could see the glow of the underwater lights shining beneath the yacht, even as the clouds of Humboldts continued to school and feed, unmolested by their larger cousins.

But Mason's smile faded as they drew near and saw the hulls of several other boats gathered around.

When the submersible broke the surface, they were greeted to the flash of emergency lights. Several Coast Guard patrol boats surrounded Mason's yacht. A police boat was pulled-up alongside.

Standing on the deck of the yacht, waving, was Ashley. Seated in a wheelchair next to her, being doctored by medics, and sporting what looked like a gunshot wound to his leg, was Professor Clyde Spencer.

Beside them, stood Lieutenant Randy Collins.

Mason's expression darkened.

Now Travis' face broke into a smile. He waved back to Ashley and Clyde as he steered the submersible their way.

CHAPTER 31

For Ashley, the next twenty-four hours were a whirlwind as the story of Colin Mason's arrest broke statewide.

Mason himself made no effort to resist being taken into custody when Travis brought the submersible to dock next to the yacht. His easy, confident demeanor never changed as Travis popped the portal and climbed out, offering his hand down to Mason, who took it congenially enough, hopping up on his one leg to where Lieutenant Collins was waiting on deck with a cadre of police and Federal officers.

"Mr. Mason," Collins said, "I've been wanting to say this to you for a long time. But you are under arrest."

Mason smiled back. "I hope it was everything you dreamed."

Then he turned to Travis.

"Well played, sir," he said, as he was cuffed and carted away by the Feds.

Travis regarded the sheets that covered what remained of Mason's men. He turned to where Clyde was nursing his bullet wound. The elderly professor was in obvious pain, but otherwise seemed in quite good-spirits.

"I might be an old bastard," Clyde said, grinning, "but I'm a tough old bastard."

For her part, Ashley couldn't believe they were all still alive. She still had Leroy's blood stained on her hands.

She spent the next two hours answering questions for the various arresting officers. By that time, the press had already gotten wind of the story and were waiting for them at the docks.

Ashley got the first taste of what was in store for her when they finally got back to shore. There was a crowd of reporters and flashing cameras, all ready to mob them, almost like packs of Humboldts themselves.

Travis and Lieutenant Collins hurried her past the TV cameras and shouting news-hounds, promising statements

133

later on. And when Ashley finally arrived home, she found a voice-message waiting from her producer.

Ashley was apparently already being made into the star. Her attack on the beach two days before had already attracted media attention, but now her producer's tone reflected a touch of awe as he ran down a list of requests from every one of the major networks, all begging for interviews.

He also quoted some extremely impressive dollar figures.

"I hope you're ready for it," he informed her, "because you have just become a commodity."

Ashley listened to the message, absorbing the implications. It seemed she was going to get her sea-monster special after all.

And she had a hell of a story to tell.

The dawn was already encroaching upon the horizon when she finally lay down in her bed and fell into a thankfully dreamless sleep.

She was awakened sometime later by a knock at her door. As she blinked the sleep out of her eyes, she realized it was full-morning.

Travis Prescott was waiting on her doorstep.

"Good morning, Ashley," he said.

He was smiling reservedly, but he looked tired, as if he'd been up all night.

"Travis," Ashley said brightly, "what's up?"

"Well," he said, "I was going to call, but I needed to stop by anyway and get my credit card back."

Ashley smiled. "I almost forgot. Please, come in."

She led him to the living room, and he sat down on her couch as she hunted for her purse, digging for his card.

"Have you seen the news yet?" Travis asked.

"No, I just woke up. My producer says the story's going viral." She smiled. "I'm going to have to do an interview with you and Clyde. After all, you're the heroes. How's his leg?"

"He's limping," Travis said. "But otherwise pretty spry. He asked about you."

Ashley handed him his card. He took it, replacing it back in his wallet.

"Ashley, we need to talk."

His tone dissolved her smile.

"Why? What's happened?"

"Colin Mason's been released."

Ashley stopped, looking back.

"What do you mean, 'released'?"

Travis shrugged.

"A judge let him out on bail in a midnight arraignment. The Feds are looking into it. The judge is already in custody."

Ashley sat down, thunderstruck.

"As near as anyone can tell," Travis said, "he's already blown town, likely skipped the States. Probably to some non-extradition country somewhere."

"So he's gone?"

Travis sighed.

"Not really *gone*," he said. "Just not *here*. And he's got a very long reach."

Ashley fell silent as Travis' words sunk in.

"I've talked to the Feds. There was some initial concern that he might go after any witnesses, but from their end, they don't view that as much of a problem because they don't *need* any testimony. You see, Mason filmed the whole thing himself with his GoPro. They've got him on video.

"And," Travis continued, "they also have his yacht. Besides the recording of what he did to his little girlfriend, they found a whole cache of videos. His 'highlight reels'. It's some pretty sick stuff. The Feds are of the opinion they have enough to put him in the Chair even if they tried him in San Francisco."

But Travis sighed, resigned.

"If it ever went to court, that is. Which, I'm told, is highly unlikely."

Travis looked at her grimly.

"The other thing you need to know," he said, "is that Lieutenant Collins has gone missing. He hasn't been seen since he left the courthouse a few hours ago. It hasn't even been a day, so he isn't even considered a missing person yet. But his wife says he never made it home."

Ashley stared back numbly. A cold finger touched her heart.

"I don't think Mason liked being arrested," Travis said.

He eyed her seriously.

"You're about to be famous," he told her. "Which means you won't be hard to find."

"You think he'll come after me?"

Travis shrugged.

"I don't know," he said. "But you need to be careful."

He stood to leave.

"What about you?" Ashley asked.

Travis smiled, resigned.

"I need to be careful too."

He turned for the door, letting himself out. As he left, he nodded back.

"Take care, Ashley. I'll keep in touch."

He shut the door behind him, leaving her sitting alone.

Ashley looked around her small rented house, where only a few short hours ago, a man had broken in, kidnapped her, and dragged her away.

She thought she had been rescued. She thought she was safe.

Now she wondered if she would ever feel safe again.

CHAPTER 32

Over the next two weeks, the squid disappeared from the waters off Beach City. As suddenly as they had appeared, the invading hordes were gone.

Ashley had been in regular contact with Travis, who had been out on the water daily. As was their way, the swarming schools of Humboldts had apparently moved on. And presumably, once the red devils were gone, the Colossals had moved on with them.

"Although," Travis said dryly, "I haven't taken the sub down over the drop-off to check."

Clyde had no particular explanation, other than to say that whatever motivation had brought them, just as abruptly caused them to leave. It was an established pattern.

"Between this year's absence of white sharks, Colin Mason, and the Kraken, it seems the California coast is now clear of apex predators," Clyde remarked. "Maybe we've earned a break."

Ashley certainly hoped so. She herself was leaving Beach City as well, and was currently spending her last night in her little rental house. She had accepted an offer from one of the major networks, who had already leased her a penthouse apartment in the city. She hadn't even seen the place except online, but from her formerly paycheck-to-paycheck lifestyle, the accommodations looked like royalty.

It occurred to her that she might actually about to be rich. It was a bit of an adjustment.

Her producer had bid her goodbye just this afternoon, actually seeming a bit choked up.

"I'm really happy for you, Ashley," he told her. Then he had smiled. "Remember us little guys."

She had filmed her own promo-spot just last week – "Hi, I'm Ashley Wells. Tune in to see me. And yadda yadda yadda."

Her first big project was to be an expansion of her sea monster special, with the difference being a budget and an expense account she had never dreamed of. She would also be filming it fully-dressed – no more string-bikini fluff.

Ashley supposed that was a good thing. She had been left with lasting scars, along all four limbs, particularly her once-shapely legs.

She remembered how Brody had told her to pass them off as tattoos.

Ashley smiled a little at the thought – bittersweet, with just a slight sting of tears.

She had already filmed a little side-piece on Brody – just a little fifteen minute featurette – and in doing so, she realized how little she'd actually known about him. The only background she could find came from Captain McCormick, who told her he'd been raised by his mother, and how she had died of cancer when he was only sixteen, and that he had been on his own ever since.

Ashley had read the online comments after the segment aired.

That was something she was already learning about being in the public eye – everyone had their two-bits, even though they didn't know you beyond a snippet of a few minutes of video. And upon this brief snapshot of your life, so were you judged. Ashley had read one post, decrying Brody as the real villain of the piece, castigating him as the reason so many people had been killed.

Ashley didn't know if that was true. He hadn't brought the red devils *or* the Krakens. And Colin Mason had been involved from the beginning. You couldn't say none of it would have happened.

Brody had also saved her life – twice – and the second time had been at the cost of his own.

And in an odd way, he had caused her dreams to come true – albeit at great cost. But wasn't that always the way of it?

Release the Kraken had put out a whole new exposé on Colossal squid, which had gone nearly as viral as had Ashley herself. She had already done multiple interviews with both Travis and Clyde, who had granted her exclusive rights.

In most facets of Ashley's life, things were looking up.

Of course, in the background, there was still the specter of Colin Mason.

Lieutenant Randy Collins had never been found. Ashley had seen his wife interviewed, tear-streaked and grief-stricken.

Ashley had not done these interviews herself. Heavy, hard-hitting journalism had never been her intention or her goal – she was a showgirl – an entertainer.

More truthfully, although she had known Collins for some time, she had never met his wife and couldn't bring herself to face her now.

Travis had remained in contact with the Feds, but so far, the word on Mason's whereabouts was mum, beyond rumors and general speculation. But leaked footage of Mason's 'highlight reels' had been released online – the shadowy areas of the dark-net – and Mason's image as a boogeyman had taken on a life of its own. No doubt a movie was pending. Ashley herself had been broached to do her own piece on Mason but had politely declined.

Travis had advised her that was likely a wise decision.

"He's still out there," he told her. "There's no reason to keep you on his mind. I suspect he wouldn't like the idea of someone profiting at his expense."

Travis also cautioned her to stay safe. Ashley assured him she would try. The penthouse the network had arranged for her was in a high-security building.

On the other hand, Mason owned cops and judges, and she doubted a security guard and a pass-code would really matter all that much.

Although that was better than the wide-open little hovel that had been her home until now. As she settled in for her last night, whatever leftover nostalgia she carried about her first house was surely tainted.

A new world awaited tomorrow. She shut off her lights and lay there in the dark, contemplating her future with a mix of excitement, anxiety and fear. Sleep was a long time in coming.

Right in the middle of the night, she suddenly came aware of hands upon her.

Ashley started to move, and realized that her wrists and ankles had been bound, and a bag had been placed over her head. As she blinked groggily, she felt the familiar soupy residue of the same sedative that had been injected into her before. She tried to call out but her mouth had been taped shut.

She could smell the salt of sea air and felt the cradle-rock of the ocean.

The grogginess of sleep fell away in a flash and she felt the ice cold rush of pure terror. As she began to struggle, the restraining hands held her firmly down.

"We got her, boss," a rough voice said, sounding so much like Leroy – and really what would be the difference?

When the bag was pulled away from her head, Ashley saw the smiling face of Colin Mason, sitting in his chair, his eyes slitted, glinting with that same obscene hunger.

Mason nodded.

Ashley was grabbed and dragged over to the railing.

In the water below, she saw the flashing red bio-luminescence of schooling Humboldts.

Ashley began to cry – it wasn't fair – Travis said they had moved on.

And then she was thrown over the side, still bound.

She hit the cold water, sucking breath through the tape strapped over her mouth...

… and then she sat up in bed with a scream.

Ashley gasped, blinking awake in terror, looking around the moonlit corners of her bedroom, her scream still wafting off the walls.

Her heart pounded in the aftermath of the dream, and cold sweat ran down her back like droplets of ice, leaving her shivering convulsively.

She sat there, panting in the dark.

It had not been her first nightmare, and it would likely not be her last.

After a few minutes, she finally began to calm. She started to rise from her bed.

That was when she heard a creak out in the hall – a floorboard that absolutely never creaked unless someone stepped on it.

She sat stone-still, waiting for a repeat of the sound.

It could have been her imagination. Or a last lingering figment from her dream.

Or...

Long minutes passed, and Ashley sat there, afraid to breathe.

Listening in the dark.

CHAPTER 33

Colin Mason sat sunning himself on the deck of his new yacht.

A hundred miles to the north was the southernmost coast of South Africa. Just a few short miles south, was the island he owned free and clear. And once at sea, he was sovereign.

He had actually owned this island for decades, but had never actually been here before. He had bought it for two reasons. The first was practical – it was a base for his operations in the southern hemisphere. He had similar islands, in various other regions, scattered all over the world.

The second reason was because these waters were famous for its large population of sharks – BIG Great Whites, specifically known for their breaching attacks, and the area was the on-site locale for many professional documentaries. He owned many of the DVDs himself.

But until this season, Mason had never needed to stray beyond California to find his white sharks. Nonetheless, he was a man who always planned ahead. And like an addict, he made sure to have a back-up source for his fix.

Even better, South Africa was cruising distance from Antarctica – the primary habitat of his newest fascination, the Colossal squid. He was already planning an expedition of his own and had, in fact, already ordered a deep-water submersible online.

In a way, this was all a lifestyle upgrade. With the local governments of the myriad countries bordering the South African coast already utterly corrupt, there was not even any need for him to operate underground. Not only that, but the local populations were so impoverished, he could hire quality help at a fraction of the cost as in the States, and they were all happy to perform any function he desired without issue or complaint.

And human life was cheap here.

Another plus was that the girl in the bikini, currently sunning topless, stretched out on the deck-recliner beside him, barely spoke any English. Certainly, *that* was an improvement. And she couldn't have been more eager to please. For her, the life aboard Mason's yacht was a dream come true.

Of course, a certain amount of rebuilding remained. Damage *had* been done to him. The States were still his biggest marketplace, and a lot of his supply-chain was currently being dismantled by the authorities.

Although, he mused, *not* by Lieutenant Collins.

No matter how he felt about his current situation, you didn't get to do that to Colin Mason.

Besides his business reconstruction, there was also the matter of his highlight reels that had been seized. Perhaps he regretted that as much as anything – it had been a treasured lifetime collection.

Although, he *had* seen that some of it was already becoming available second-hand online. Clearly, he wasn't the only one who indulged such tastes.

But like anything, it could be rebuilt.

Currently, he had his new crew of mercs chumming the water, and already there were several large Great Whites circling the boat.

Mason watched the massive fish cruising back and forth, chomping at the bits of flotsam, his eyes dreamy with fascination. As it always did, his hand strayed to the nub of his hip, just above his missing leg.

He glanced at the nubile young thing lying topless beside him.

"Hey, girl," he said, with his cat's grin, "come look at this."

With the same obedient eagerness with which she dropped down on her knees, the girl – whose name Mason still hadn't quite learned to pronounce – joined him by the railing.

His hand touched her shoulder, caressing gently and disarmingly, as she stared down at the circling fins below.

Mason was eager for his submersible to come in. He couldn't wait to launch his first expedition after Colossal squid.

But in the meantime, he still had his sharks.

Mason sat watching the circling predators – so serene, so perfect – so utterly and unabashedly deadly – and he thought about people on the other side of the world who had crossed him.

All in due course, he thought. Give them time. Let them feel safe.

He rubbed his hand on the young girl's shoulder and she sighed contentedly, as if with not a care in the world.

With his eyes silt like a cat's, agleam with vile, predatory hunger, Colin Mason smiled.

THE END

Check out other great

Sea Monster Novels!

Robert J. Stava

NEPTUNES RECKONING

At the easternmost end of Long Island lies a seaside town known as Montauk. Ground Zero on the Eastern seaboard for all manner of conspiracy theories involving it's hidden Cold War military base, rumors of time-travel experiments and alien visitors... For renowned Naval historian William Vanek it's the where his grandfather's ship went down on a Top Secret mission during WWII code-named "Neptune's Reckoning". Together with Marine Biologist Daniel Cheung and disgraced French underwater explorer Arnaud Navarre, he's about to discover the truth behind the urban legends: a nightmare from beyond space and time that has been reawakened by global warming and toxic dumping, a nightmare the government tried to keep submerged. Neptune's Reckoning. Terror knows no depth

Bestselling collection

DEAD BAIT

A husband hell-bent on revenge hunts a Wereshark... A Russian mail order bride with a fishy secret... Crabs with a collective consciousness... A vampire who transforms into a Candiru... Zombie piranha...Bait that will have you crawling out of your skin and more. Drawing on horror, humor with a helping of dark fantasy and a touch of deviance, these 19 contemporary stories pay homage to the monsters that lurk in the murky waters of our imaginations. If you thought it was safe to go back in the water... Think Again!

Check out other great

Sea Monster Novels!

Michael Cole

MEGALODON VS COLOSSAL SNAKE

Brought to life by the miracle of DNA cloning, a 93-foot Megalodon shark has escaped captivity. With an insatiable appetite and unmatched aggression, it travels west for the Georgia coast, leaving a path of destruction in its wake. Bullets and harpoons can't penetrate it, steel nets can't hold it, and it's only a matter of time before the whole world finds out about it. In a race to stop the beast, the organization responsible recruit a marine biologist and a herpetologist to develop a plan to catch it. To do it, they must unleash the company's other genetically modified experiment—a 150-foot snake, resurrected from the DNA of the mighty Titanoboa. The pursuit leads to inevitable combat, and the scientists are forced to witness the deadly realities of genetic tampering. As the battle escalates, it is clear nobody is safe...and that nature never intended for these beasts to return. As the destruction mounts, and the death toll climbs, the true loser of Megalodon vs. Colossal Snake is humanity.

Tim Waggoner

TEETH OF THE SEA

They glide through dark waters, sleek and silent as death itself. Ancient predators with only two desires – to feed and reproduce. They've traveled to the resort island of Las Dagas to do both, and the guests make tempting meals. The humans are on land, though, out of reach. But the resort's main feature is an intricate canal system . . . . . . and it's starting to rain.